AMERICA'S STORY

Historical Sources on the Civil Rights Movement

CHET'LA SEBREE AND ELIZABETH SIRIMARCO

Cavendish Square
New York

Published in 2020 by Cavendish Square Publishing, LLC
243 5th Avenue, Suite 136, New York, NY 10016

First Edition

Library of Congress Cataloging-in-Publication Data

Names: Sebree, Chet'la, author. | Sirimarco, Elizabeth, 1966- author.
Title: Historical Sources on the Civil Rights Movement / Chet'la Sebree and Elizabeth Sirimarco.
Description: First edition. | New York : Cavendish Square, 2020. |
Series: America's story | Includes bibliographical references and index.
Identifiers: LCCN 2018031741 (print) | LCCN 2018036841 (ebook) |
ISBN 9781502640918 (ebook) | ISBN 9781502640901 (library bound) | ISBN 9781502640895 (pbk.)
Subjects: LCSH: African Americans--Civil rights--Juvenile literature. |
African Americans--Civil rights--Sources--Juvenile literature. |
Civil rights movements--United States--Juvenile literature. |
Civil rights movements--United States--Sources--Juvenile literature. |
United States--Race relations--Juvenile literature. |
United States--Race relations--Sources--Juvenile literature.
Classification: LCC E185.61 (ebook) | LCC E185.61 .S399 2019 (print) | DDC 323.1196/073--dc23
LC record available at https://lccn.loc.gov/2018031741

Editorial Director: David McNamara
Copy Editor: Nathan Heidelberger
Associate Art Director: Alan Sliwinski
Designer: Christina Shults
Production Coordinator: Karol Szymczuk
Photo Research: J8 Media

The photographs in this book are used by permission and through the courtesy of:
Cover, p 21 Everett Historical/Shutterstock.com, (background and used throughout) Foxstudio/Shutterstock.com; p. 4, 36, 48, 74, 78, 83, 86, 94, 110, 121 Bettmann Archive/Getty Images; p. 8 The Print Collector/Getty Images; p. 13, 107 Paul Schutzer/The LIFE Picture Collection/Getty Images; p. 14, 25 Library of Congress; p. 17 History and Art Collection/Alamy Stock Photo; p. 28 Frances Benjamin Johnston/Library of Congress/Wikimedia Commons/File:Booker T. Washington by Francis Benjamin Johnston, c. 1895.jpg/Public Doman; p. 31 Mary Garrity/Wikimedia Commons/File:Mary Garrity Ida B. WellsBarnett/Google Art Project restoration Crop.jpg/Public Domain; p. 43 Boston City Council/Wikimedia Commons/File:WMTrotter1915.jpg/Public Domain; p. 54 Thomas D. Mcavoy/The LIFE Picture Collection/Getty Images; p. 61 Keystone/Getty Images; p. 64 Carl Iwasaki/The LIFE Images Collection/Getty Images; p. 69 Universal History Archive/Getty Images; p. 71 Grey Villet/The LIFE Picture Collection/Getty Images; p. 80 Central Press/Getty Images; p. 98 Afro American Newspapers/Gado/Getty Images; p. 105 John Loengard/The LIFE Picture Collection/Getty Images; p. 108 The Birmingham News/AP Images; p. 128 Mondadori Portfolio/Getty Images.

Printed in the United States of America

AMERICA'S STORY

CONTENTS

In June 1963, over one hundred thousand people marched in the Detroit Walk to Freedom. At the event, Martin Luther King Jr. delivered an early version of his "I Have a Dream" speech.

Primary Sources

In the pages that follow, you will hear from many different people from a time in America's past. These selections will vary in length. Some are long, and others are short. You'll find many easy to understand at first reading, but some may require several readings. All the selections have one thing in common, however. They are primary sources. They are important to us because they are the core material for all historical investigation.

What Is a Primary Source?

The term "primary source" is the name historians give to the information that makes up the record of human existence. A primary source is "history" itself. Primary sources are evidence. They give historians the all-important clues they need to understand the past.

Perhaps you have read a detective story in which an investigator has to solve a mystery by piecing together bits of evidence that he or she uncovers. The detective makes deductions, or educated guesses based on the evidence, and solves the mystery once all the deductions point in a certain direction. Historians work in much the same way. Like detectives, they analyze data through careful reading and rereading. After much analysis, they draw conclusions about an event, a person, or an entire era. Different historians may analyze the same evidence and come to different conclusions. That is why there is often strong disagreement about an event.

Primary sources are also called documents. It is a rather dry word to describe what can be just about anything: an official speech by a government leader, an old map, an act of Congress, a letter, a diary entry, a newspaper article, a song, a poster, a cartoon, a photograph, or someone captured on tape or film.

By examining the following primary sources, you will be taking on the role of historian. Here is a chance to jump into an important era of US history—the civil rights movement. You will come to know the stories of the men and women who lived through this challenging period. You will read the words of the movement's leaders and of ordinary citizens, of activists and journalists and protesters.

How to Read a Primary Source

Each document in this book deals with the civil rights movement. Some of the documents are from government archives such as presidential libraries. Others are from the writings and speeches of major figures in the movement, such as Ida B. Wells and W. E. B. Du Bois, Thurgood Marshall and Fannie Lou Hamer, Martin Luther King Jr. and Malcolm X. Other documents are taken from memoirs and newspaper articles. All of the documents, major and minor, help us to understand what it was like to live during the civil rights movement.

The selections you will read may be difficult to understand at first. There will be a variety of styles, from very formal to quite informal. Don't be afraid. Interpreting these kinds of documents is exactly the sort of work a historian does.

As you read each document, ask yourself some basic questions. Who is writing or speaking? Who is that person's intended audience? What is he or she trying to tell the audience? Is the message clearly expressed or is it implied, or stated indirectly? What words does the writer use to convey his or her message? Are the words emotional or neutral in tone? These are questions that can help you think critically about a primary source.

There are also some tools in each chapter to help you unpack these documents. Some terms and concepts you may not be familiar with have been explained in sidebars. Also, questions follow each of the documents to help you focus and think through the primary source you have just read. As you read each selection, you'll probably come up with many questions of your own. That's great! The work of a historian always leads to many, many questions. Some can be answered, while others will require more investigation.

Racial inequality in the United States dates back to slavery, which began in 1619 in the British colonies.

INTRODUCTION

The Long Struggle

In 1619, twenty Africans were brought to the British settlement of Jamestown, Virginia. These Africans would be the first sold into slavery in colonial America. Over the next 250 years, hundreds of thousands would follow. These Africans did not come by choice. Torn from their homes and families, they arrived starving, stripped nearly bare, and in chains. They were thrust into a life of slavery in a strange land. It was not until the mid-nineteenth century that enslaved Africans were freed from bondage. Although the unjust practice of slavery had been outlawed, African Americans would continue to struggle to be seen and treated equally.

Federal Protection of Citizens' Rights

After the long history of slavery in the United States, the institution was finally brought to an end by the Civil War (1861–1865). The war had divided the slaveholding South and the predominantly free North. The Southern states had attempted to secede, or withdraw, from the United States, also called the Union, and form a separate country, the Confederate States of America. The North, under the leadership of President Abraham Lincoln, fought to preserve the Union.

The aftermath of the Civil War thrust the United States into a difficult period: the Reconstruction Era. United again as a single nation, the North and the South had to find a way to overcome the serious issues that had divided them. One of the most challenging questions was the status of those who were previously enslaved. They were now considered US citizens. Citizenship meant that they had the same civil rights, or personal freedoms, guaranteed by law to other American citizens. However, the country had to determine how to protect these rights in the face of deeply rooted racism and prejudice. During the Reconstruction Era, Congress passed three amendments to the US Constitution with these issues in mind.

The new amendments, often called the Reconstruction Amendments, promised freedom and equal rights to all US citizens. The Thirteenth Amendment abolished slavery. The Fourteenth Amendment promises the rights of citizenship to all people born in the United States, in addition to those who undergo the process to become a citizen. These rights include, among others, freedom of speech, freedom of religion, and the right to gather peacefully for political or other purposes. The Fourteenth Amendment also provides equal protection of said rights and prohibits individual states from taking them away. Finally, the Fifteenth Amendment grants suffrage, or the right to vote, to black men. Women of all races would not be permitted to vote until 1920. Once passed, the amendments became federal law and could be enforced by Congress.

To give the federal government more power to protect black citizens, Congress passed the Civil Rights Act of 1875.

This legislation, or law, was intended to ensure that all African Americans, regardless of former status as enslaved or free, would have equal access to public facilities. The act promised that all citizens were "entitled to the full and equal enjoyment of the accommodations, advantages, facilities, and privileges of inns, public conveyances on land or water, theaters, and other places of public amusement."

Congress hoped that the new law, along with the amendments, would be enough to protect the rights of black Americans. It was not.

The "Free" South

During the early years of Reconstruction, representatives from the North ran governments in the Southern states. They made sure that the amendments were not violated. Black Americans participated eagerly in the democratic process. They exercised their right to vote and held public office at all levels of government, from local councils to the US Congress. Additionally, federal troops were stationed in the South to protect the formerly enslaved and restore order. Similarly, the Freedmen's Bureau, a federal agency focused on helping those affected by slavery and the Civil War, provided protection. However, life returned to normal when Northern representatives left the South and the government withdrew troops.

Many white Southerners quickly found ways to resist and defy the laws. They made it difficult for black Southerners to find decent work to support their families. Terrorist groups such as the Ku Klux Klan used violence to keep black men from voting or participating in politics. State legislatures, or governing bodies, created laws to sidestep the amendments and the Civil Rights Act. Some states, for example, allowed only landowners and people who could read to vote. Not many people who were previously enslaved were fortunate enough to own land. Similarly, many did not know how to read since laws had long restricted free people from teaching enslaved people to read or write.

The "Free" North

Moving to the North offered little more opportunity. Few Northerners truly viewed African Americans as equal citizens. Working-class white people disliked the African Americans' arrival. They feared black people would take away their jobs. Policies, official or simply understood, often kept black people from living in white neighborhoods or attending the best schools.

African Americans across the nation faced racism and discrimination. They had won freedom, but the country that claimed to be the greatest democracy in the world provided them little opportunity.

The Beginning of the Movement

Many Americans consider the civil rights movement, or the organized struggle for justice and equality, to have happened in the 1950s and 1960s. However, the story of civil rights began long before that significant chapter in US history. There were those, like Ida B. Wells and W. E. B. Du Bois, who began the struggle in the late nineteenth century. They deserve just as much credit for the great strides they made toward equality as Thurgood Marshall and Martin Luther King Jr.

The story of civil rights in America is not an easy one to recount. The road to equal treatment has been a long, troublesome one. It is a story of courage and violence, strength and hatred. People involved in the movement often put themselves and those they loved at risk for the fight for equal rights. The effects of their sacrifices still echo into today. Similarly, the struggle still continues.

The civil rights movement often involved violence. Sometimes police and troops were brought in to protect African Americans as they fought for equality and freedom. However, there were times where these same officials mistreated black people as they fought for their rights.

Jim Crow is a character often depicted as simple-minded. He became a caricature of how white people perceived black people in the nineteenth and early twentieth centuries.

1 The Jim Crow Era

In 1828, Thomas Dartmouth ("Daddy") Rice started performing the minstrel routine "Jump Jim Crow." Minstrel shows were an American theatrical genre popular in the nineteenth and early twentieth centuries. Blackface minstrelsy, intended to be comedic, were shows based on the portrayal of racial stereotypes. They were known for white minstrel performers painting their faces black and pretending to be enslaved Africans. These shows negatively portrayed black people. Rice was "the father of the blackface show." It is unlikely that he knew when he developed the routine that the words "Jim Crow" would become part of the fabric of US history.

Failed Federal Protections

The federal government passed the Reconstruction Amendments and the Civil Rights Act of 1875 to protect former slaves, but these measures were largely ineffective.

As Northerners withdrew from the South after Reconstruction, Southerners created city and state laws to restrict black people's rights. Additionally, these laws restricted African Americans' access to both public and private facilities. For instance, these laws affected everything from restaurants and libraries to neighborhoods and churches.

This system of laws and customs often supported segregation, or the separation of a race, class, or other group by means of discriminatory laws and policies. Across America, these laws were known as Jim Crow laws. Although Rice's show is credited for the "Jim Crow" language, no one is sure how the name came to be used in this context.

As the nineteenth century came to a close, it was clear that black people were considered second-class citizens. The government had not done enough to secure their civil rights, and it would do even less in the coming years.

Legal Segregation

In 1883, the Supreme Court decided that the Civil Rights Act was unconstitutional, or illegal based on the laws outlined by the US Constitution. Then, in 1896, the court upheld a Louisiana state law that segregated train cars. It was a landmark decision, solidifying a new legal principle and giving official protection to Jim Crow laws around the country. The court's justices stated that as long as black people had access to "equal" facilities, then laws separating races were legal. This idea became known as the "separate but equal" principle. It would be the law of the land from the late 1800s until the 1960s.

Across the country were vivid reminders that black people were second-class citizens. Signs that read "Whites Only" or "Colored," a now offensive term used to describe black people, hung over water fountains and above doors to restrooms, restaurants, and theaters. Employers and landlords found ways to restrict black people from the best opportunities and housing. Businesses refused to serve black customers. Over time, fewer and fewer black men cast their votes in elections. They were discouraged either by rules and regulations or by threats and intimidation. For black people, freedom had proved difficult to achieve and enjoy.

The *Plessy v. Ferguson* Decision

In 1890, Louisiana passed the Separate Car Act. The law stated that all railway companies had to provide "equal but separate" cars for white and black people. Passengers who sat in the wrong train car faced a twenty-five-dollar fine or twenty days in jail.

In 1892, a thirty-one-year-old shoemaker named Homer Plessy took a seat in a car for white passengers in New Orleans. When he refused to leave, he was arrested. Plessy decided to take his case to court, stating that the Separate Car Act violated his Fourteenth

This cartoon illustrates how the "separate but equal" principle often led to unequal conditions for black people.

Amendment rights. The amendment provides equal protection under the law to all citizens.

Louisiana judge John H. Ferguson ruled against him, but Plessy challenged Ferguson's decision all the way to the US Supreme Court. All but one of the justices decided the law was constitutional. The majority opinion, or the written explanation for the decision in the case, set the "separate but equal" standard. It legalized segregation so long as African Americans were provided with facilities equal to the ones provided to white people. Oftentimes, however, the facilities were not in fact equal.

> The object of the [fourteenth] amendment was undoubtedly to enforce the absolute equality of the two races before the law, but ... it could not have been intended to abolish distinctions based upon color, or to enforce social, as distinguished from political, equality, or a commingling of the two races upon terms unsatisfactory to either. Laws permitting, and even requiring, their separation, in places where they are liable to be brought into contact, do not necessarily imply the inferiority of either race.
>
> We consider the underlying fallacy of the plaintiff's [Plessy's] argument to consist in the assumption that the enforced separation of the two races stamps the colored race with a badge of inferiority. If this be so, it is not by reason of anything found in the act, but solely because the colored race chooses to put that construction upon it ... The argument also assumes

that social prejudices may be overcome by legislation, and that equal rights cannot be secured to the negro except by an enforced commingling of the two races. We cannot accept this proposition. If the two races are to meet upon terms of social equality, it must be the result of natural affinities ... Legislation is powerless to eradicate racial instincts, or to abolish distinctions based upon physical differences, and the attempt to do so can only result in accentuating the difficulties of the present situation. If the civil and political rights of both races be equal, one cannot be inferior to the other civilly ... or politically. If one race be inferior to the other socially, the Constitution of the United States cannot put them upon the same plane.

—From US Supreme Court, *Plessy v. Ferguson,* 163 U.S. 537 (1896).

CONSIDER THIS

1. The majority opinion states there is a difference between social equality and political equality. What does this mean? Do you think it's possible to have one form of equality without the other?
2. The justices say that laws cannot "eradicate racial instincts"—in other words, laws cannot end prejudice. Do you believe this is true?
3. Who do you think was in charge of deciding what was considered "equal"?

KEY TERMS AND CONCEPTS

From the *Plessy v. Ferguson* majority opinion:

accentuate To make more apparent.

affinities Positive feelings, especially based on a sense of similarity.

badge of inferiority Second-class citizenship.

commingling Mixing or blending.

construction Belief or interpretation.

eradicate To get rid of.

fallacy A false belief.

instincts Prejudices.

liable Likely.

plaintiff A person who brings a case against another person.

plane Level of social status.

proposition An idea or suggestion offered for discussion.

From Justice Harlan's dissenting opinion:

caste A system that divides people into different classes.

indissolubly linked Connected forever.

perpetuate To maintain.

prestige General admiration.

sanction of law Legal permission or approval.

state enactments State laws.

Justice Harlan Dissents

John Marshall Harlan served on the US Supreme Court from 1877 until he died in 1911.

Only one justice, a Southerner named John Marshall Harlan, disagreed with the *Plessy* decision. He wrote a dissenting opinion, or a written statement that disagrees with the court's decision. Harlan believed that the court made racial prejudice acceptable with its decision. "The thin disguise of 'equal' accommodations … will not mislead anyone," wrote Harlan. In other words, he thought the justices created a poor veil for legalizing inequality and racism. Harlan's words proved to be true. From restaurants and schools to theaters and drinking fountains, segregation became a way of life.

> The white race deems itself to be the dominant race in this country. And so it is, in prestige, in achievements, in education, in wealth and in power … But in view of the Constitution, in the eye of the law, there is in this country no superior, dominant, ruling class of citizens. There is no caste here. Our Constitution is color-blind, and neither knows nor tolerates classes among citizens. In respect of civil rights, all citizens are equal before the law. The humblest is the peer of the most powerful. The law regards man as man, and takes no account of his surroundings or of his color when his civil rights as guaranteed by the supreme law of the land are involved …

CONSIDER THIS

1. How do you think people argued that the schools for white and black children were equal?

KEY TERMS AND CONCEPTS

From Ray Sprigle's article:

clapboards Thin, overlapping pieces of wood.

cross-ventilation Air moving across the room.

dilapidated In a state of disrepair.

furnish To provide.

hypocrisy The state of saying one thing but doing the other; contradiction.

From James Weldon Johnson's novel:

countenance Face or facial expression.

degeneracy The state of having declined below the normal standard of existence; a term sometimes used by white people to describe people of other races as "less than" or "subhuman."

railroad tie A part of a railroad track that keeps the rails upright and appropriately spaced.

Fair Trial vs. Lynch Mobs

Among the most significant rights of American citizens is the right to a fair trial. After the war, a practice called lynching became a popular way for white people to handle black people they suspected of committing a crime. Lynching is the execution, primarily by hanging, of a person without giving him or her a fair trial.

Black people knew that they could become victims of lynching at any time, even if they were innocent of any wrongdoing. All it might take was the accusation of a white person. Lynch mobs of white people kidnapped and murdered black people. These often innocent black Americans were hanged, burned, and often tortured as well.

It is hard to know how many people were victims of this practice because many cases went unreported. However, researchers conclude that nearly four thousand black people were lynched between 1877 and 1950.

The following passage is a fictional account of a lynching. It is from *The Autobiography of an Ex-Coloured Man*, the story of a man whose light skin allows him to pass for white.

> A space was quickly cleared in the crowd, and a rope placed about his neck, when from somewhere came the suggestion, "Burn him!" It ran like an electric current. Have you ever witnessed the transformation of human beings into savage beasts? Nothing can be more terrible. A railroad tie

Author of *The Autobiography of an Ex-Coloured Man*, James Weldon Johnson was also a poet, songwriter, and diplomat.

was sunk into the ground, the rope was removed, and a chain brought and securely coiled round the victim and the stake. There he stood, a man only in form and stature, every sign of degeneracy stamped upon his countenance. His eyes were dull and vacant, indicating not a single ray of thought. Evidently the realization of his fearful fate had robbed him of whatever reasoning power he had ever possessed. He was too stunned and stupefied even to tremble. Fuel was brought from everywhere, oil, the torch; the flames crouched for an instant as though to gather strength, then leaped up as high as their victim's head. He squirmed, he writhed, strained at his chains, then gave out cries and groans that I shall always hear. The cries and groans were choked off by the fire and smoke; but his eyes, bulging from the sockets, rolled from side to side, appealing in vain for help. Some of the crowd yelled and cheered, others seemed appalled at what they had done, and there were those who turned away sickened at the sight. I was fixed to the spot where I stood, powerless to take my eyes from what I did not want to see ... A great wave of humiliation and shame swept over me. Shame that I belonged to a race that could be so dealt with.

—From James Weldon Johnson, *The Autobiography of an Ex-Coloured Man* (New York: Vintage Books, 1927). First published anonymously in 1912.

CONSIDER THIS

1. Can you think of reasons white Southerners might have lynched black people rather than allow the law to determine whether these people were guilty or innocence?
2. Why does the narrator of this passage say he felt shame? Why do you think he couldn't look away?

A Divide

Once Jim Crow laws were in place, many African Americans felt injustice and prejudice were facts of life that couldn't be changed. Some believed that fighting the oppressive situation would cause trouble. To be seen as a troublemaker was dangerous, so many suffered in silence. Others, however, wanted to find new avenues and ways for black people to improve their lives.

Born enslaved in 1856, Booker T. Washington would become one of the most influential black reformers and educators in the late nineteenth and early twentieth centuries.

2 *Early Activism*

Booker T. Washington was an educator and advocate for change. He did not, however, believe in protest. He actually thought black people should abandon their hopes for civil rights and should tolerate racial discrimination and segregation, for a time. Instead of protesting, he believed African Americans should focus on developing agricultural and industrial skills. With this in mind, he opened a school, the Tuskegee Normal and Industrial Institute, in Macon County, Alabama.

The Tuskegee Institute

The institute was a school in which African Americans could gain a practical education such as skills in farming, mechanics, and housekeeping. The institute encouraged students to learn work-based skills, setting aside civil rights activism and intellectual pursuits in favor of economic improvement. Washington believed that once economic security was achieved, then black people would earn respect from white people. This, Washington promised, would lead to improved relations between the races. He believed civil rights would eventually follow.

A Different Approach

Washington was considered one of the most influential black leaders of his day. Both white and black people admired the work he did. However, some African Americans did not agree with his strategy of acceptance, especially at a time of increasing segregation and violence against black people.

These individuals believed it was wrong to limit gifted and intelligent African Americans to simple, unsatisfying jobs because of their race. These activists, or people who try to bring about social or political change, were the earliest leaders of what would become the civil rights movement. They believed the only way to end discrimination, racism, and prejudice was to fight these evils head-on.

Ida B. Wells: *A Red Record*

Ida B. Wells was one of these fearless early activists. She was a journalist and editor of the *Memphis Free Speech* newspaper in Tennessee. In 1892, she investigated the lynching of three black storeowners who had been accused of attacking a white woman. She concluded that the men had not committed the crime. She wrote that these men lost their lives because they were taking business away from the white owner of another store.

When she published her findings, white people were outraged. Her article called into question the most common excuse that Southerners gave for lynching someone. Black men were often lynched as punishment for attacking white women. In response to her article, angry white people destroyed the *Free Speech* office.

Ida B. Wells, who took the name Wells-Barnett after marriage, was not only a journalist but also an activist in the antilynching, early civil rights, and women's suffrage movements.

Wells took shelter in the North, where she continued to write about anti-black violence and discrimination. In her 1895 pamphlet *A Red Record*, she gave a brief history of lynching. She then tallied the number of lynchings that had occurred in 1893. She's responsible for some of the first statistics we have on lynching. She also offered compassionate white readers suggestions on ways to stop the practice of lynching. Wells's work contributed to the anti-lynching movement, a cause that would soon be taken up by women of both races, North and South.

> During the slave regime, the Southern white man owned the Negro body and soul. It was to his interest to dwarf the soul and preserve the body. Vested with unlimited power over his slave, to subject him to any and all kinds of physical punishment, the white man was still restrained from such punishment as tended to injure the slave by abating his physical powers and thereby reducing his financial worth. While slaves were scourged mercilessly, and in countless cases inhumanly treated in other respects, still the white owner rarely permitted his anger to go so far as to take a life, which would entail upon him a loss of several hundred dollars. The slave was rarely killed, he was too valuable ...
>
> But Emancipation came and the vested interests of the white man in the Negro's body were lost. The white man had no right to scourge the emancipated Negro, still less has he a right to kill him ... In slave times the Negro was kept subservient and submissive by the frequency and severity of the scourging, but, with freedom, a new system of intimidation came into vogue; the Negro was not only whipped and scourged; he was killed ...

> Not all nor nearly all of the murders done by white men, during the past thirty years [1865–1895] in the South have come to light, but the statistics as gathered and preserved by white men, and which have not been questioned, show that during these years more than ten thousand Negroes have been killed in cold blood, without the formality of judicial trial and legal execution. And yet ... the same record shows that during all these years, and for all these murders only three white men have been tried, convicted, and executed.
>
> —From Ida B. Wells, *A Red Record,* 1895. Reprinted in Jacqueline Jones Royster, ed., Southern *Horrors and Other Writings: The Anti-Lynching Campaign of Ida B. Wells, 1892–1900* (Boston: Bedford Books, 1997).

CONSIDER THIS

1. According to Wells, why were black people rarely punished with death when slavery was still legal?
2. Wells notes that few white men were ever punished for lynching. What explanation can you give for this?

W. E. B. Du Bois's Opinion of Booker T. Washington

A writer, an intellectual, and a social scientist, W. E. B. Du Bois is considered one of the most influential African Americans prior to the modern civil rights movement. Du Bois was the first African American to earn a PhD from Harvard University. Once out of school, he began to conduct research on the lives of black Americans. As he pursued his work, Du Bois realized he "could

KEY TERMS AND CONCEPTS

From Ida B. Wells's *A Red Record*:

abate To decrease.

convict To find someone guilty of a crime.

dwarf To make small or to diminish.

entail To involve.

scourge To whip.

several hundred dollars A hundred dollars in the 1890s would be worth about $2,600 in 2018.

vested Given by law.

vogue Popularity.

From W. E. B. Du Bois's "Of Mr. Booker T. Washington and Others":

conciliation The act of stopping someone from being angry.

disenfranchisement The loss of the right to vote, or more broadly, the loss of the privileges afforded to citizens of a society.

environing Surrounding.

impress To stress an idea.

insistently Firmly.

pessimistic Seeing the worst of things.

potent Having power or influence.

propaganda Information or advertisement used to promote a political agenda.

proposition An idea or suggestion offered for discussion.

sinister Evil.

not be a calm, cool, and detached scientist while Negroes were lynched, murdered, and starved." Increasingly, he began to speak out about injustice.

In 1903, he published a collection of essays, *The Souls of Black Folk*. In it, Du Bois said that the "color line," or racial segregation, was the most serious problem the United States would face in the twentieth century. One of the essays, "Of Mr. Booker T. Washington and Others," evaluates others who were a part of the movement.

> Mr. Washington distinctly asks that black people give up, at least for the present, three things,—
>
> First, political power,
>
> Second, insistence on civil rights,
>
> Third, higher education of Negro youth,—and concentrate all their energies on industrial education, and accumulation of wealth, and the conciliation of the South. This policy has been courageously and insistently advocated for over fifteen years ... In these years there have occurred:
>
> 1. The disfranchisement of the Negro.
>
> 2. The legal creation of a distinct status of civil inferiority for the Negro.
>
> 3. The steady withdrawal of aid from institutions for the higher training of the Negro.

William Edward Burghardt (W. E. B.) Du Bois, an activist, author, sociologist, and historian, was committed to the fight for equality in the early twentieth century. His book *The Souls of Black Folk* remains one of the most important contributions to African American literature.

These movements are not, to be sure, direct results of Mr. Washington's teachings; but his propaganda has, without a shadow of doubt, helped their speedier accomplishment …

It would be unjust to Mr. Washington not to acknowledge that in several instances he has opposed movements in the South which were unjust to the Negro; … he has spoken against lynching, and in other ways has openly or silently set his influence against sinister schemes and unfortunate happenings. Notwithstanding this, it is equally true to assert that on the whole the distinct impression left by Mr. Washington's propaganda is, first, that the South is justified in its present attitude toward the Negro because of the Negro's degradation; secondly, that the prime cause of the Negro's failure to rise more quickly is his wrong education in the past; and, thirdly, that his future rise depends primarily on his own efforts. Each of these propositions is a dangerous half-truth. . . . [F]irst, slavery and race-prejudice are potent if not sufficient causes of the Negro's position; second, industrial and common-school training were necessarily slow in planting because they had to await the black teachers trained by higher institutions … and, third, while it is a great truth to say that the Negro must strive and strive mightily to help himself, it is equally true that unless his striving be not simply seconded, but rather aroused and encouraged, by the initiative of the richer and wiser environing group, he cannot hope for great success.

In his failure to realize and impress this last point, Mr. Washington is especially to be criticised. His doctrine has tended to make the whites, North and South, shift the burden of the Negro problem to the Negro's shoulders and stand aside as critical and rather pessimistic spectators; when in fact the burden belongs to the nation, and the hands of none of us are clean if we bend not our energies to righting these great wrongs.

—From W.E.B. Du Bois, "Of Mr. Booker T. Washington and Others," in *The Souls of Black Folk* (Cambridge, Massachusetts: A. C. McClurg & Co., 1903).

CONSIDER THIS

1. Du Bois believed the increasing hostility between white and black people would be the biggest problem Americans would face in the twentieth century. According to this essay, how had Booker T. Washington contributed to this problem?
2. What does Du Bois claim had caused "the Negro's degradation"?
3. Washington believed that African Americans were responsible for their own lives and futures. What was Du Bois's viewpoint on this issue?

The Origins of the NAACP

In 1908, horrified by a race riot in Springfield, Illinois, a group of black and white activists organized a meeting to discuss racism. Sixty people attended and later signed the Platform of the National Negro Committee. This committee would soon become an organization called the National Association for the Advancement of Colored People, also known as the NAACP. Only a handful of the sixty people who signed the document were African Americans. Among those were prominent leaders. These leaders included Ida B. Wells, W. E. B. Du Bois, and educator and activist Mary Church Terrell.

The organization was focused on ensuring and protecting equal rights for everyone. It grew quickly in its first decade. By 1919, the NAACP would have around ninety thousand members and three hundred local branches.

Unlike Booker T. Washington, members of the NAACP were unwilling to wait for things to get better. They demanded change. Through court battles and protests, they would work to ensure that black citizens' rights were protected. The following is the National Negro Committee platform (later adopted by the NAACP), which was signed on February 12, 1909.

> We denounce the ever-growing oppression of our 10,000,000 colored fellow citizens as the greatest menace that threatens the country. Often plundered of their just share of the public funds, robbed of nearly all part in the government, segregated by common carriers, some murdered … , and all treated with open contempt by officials, they are held in some States in practical slavery to the white community. The systematic persecution of law-abiding citizens and their disfranchisement on account of their race alone is a crime that will ultimately drag down to an infamous end any nation that allows it to be practiced …
>
> We agree fully with the prevailing opinion that the transformation of the unskilled colored laborers in industry and agriculture into skilled workers is of vital importance to that race and to the nation, but we demand for the Negroes, as for all others, a free and

complete education, whether by city, State or nation, a grammar school and industrial training for all and technical, professional, and academic education for the most gifted.

But ... the Negro ... will never receive a fair and equal treatment until he is given equal treatment in the Legislature and before the law. Nor will the practically educated Negro, no matter how valuable to the community he may prove, be given a fair return for his labor or encouraged to put forth his best efforts or given the chance to develop that efficiency that comes only outside the school until he is respected in his legal rights as ... a citizen ...

As first and immediate steps toward remedying these national wrongs, ... we demand of Congress and the Executive:

(1) That the Constitution be strictly enforced and the civil rights guaranteed under the Fourteenth Amendment be secured impartially to all.

(2) That there be equal educational opportunities for all and in all the States, and that public school expenditure be the same for the Negro and white child.

(3) That in accordance with the Fifteenth Amendment the right of the Negro to the ballot on the same terms as other citizens be recognized in every part of the country.

—Platform Adopted by the National Negro Committee, 1909.

KEY TERMS AND CONCEPTS

From the National Negro Committee platform:

denounce To declare publicly as wrong.

expenditure The amount of money spent.

menace A threat.

persecution Poor treatment, especially because of religion, politics, or race.

plunder To steal, usually by force or violence.

prevailing The most popular or influential.

treated with open contempt Disregarded or looked down upon.

From the *New York Times* article:

auditor An observer.

blackmail The use of threats to force someone into doing something.

cross-examine To aggressively question someone.

delegation A group of representatives.

designate To assign.

inaugurate To initiate or start.

resent To feel bitter about something or someone.

From Claude McCay's explanation:

gaily Cheerfully.

morbid Unpleasant, often dealing with death or disease.

sore Distressed or painful.

speakeasy An illegal bar or nightclub during Prohibition, a time in the United States when it was illegal to produce or sell alcoholic beverages (1920–1933).

World War World War I (1914–1918).

CONSIDER THIS

1. What is meant by the term "practical slavery"?
2. How does the platform address the beliefs of Booker T. Washington? Does it support Washington's ideas? Does it differ from the educator's views?

A Heated Debate at the White House

William Monroe Trotter was a Harvard-educated activist and the editor of a Boston newspaper for African Americans, the *Guardian*. Trotter had supported Democratic candidate Woodrow Wilson in the election of 1912. However, the new president's actions would sorely disappoint him. President Wilson created segregation policies for the US government. For instance, he created rules prohibiting black and white postal clerks from working together.

In 1914, Trotter wrote a letter requesting a meeting with the president. Wilson agreed. Trotter arrived at the White House with a small group of black activists. The two men argued heatedly for forty-five minutes before Trotter and his companions were escorted out of the White House. Trotter was banned from returning for the rest of Wilson's term. When Trotter left the building, he spoke to reporters about what had happened. The excerpt below is taken from an article that appeared on the front page of the *New York Times* the following day.

> Washington, Nov. 12—Segregation of white and negro civil service employees in Government departments, a system inaugurated during the present Administration, is to be continued.

William Monroe Trotter was a writer and an advocate for racial equality. Like Du Bois, he criticized Booker T. Washington's approach to the injustices black people faced.

President Wilson made clear his views on the subject today when he received a delegation representing the National Independence Equal Rights League. The President resented the attitude of the spokesman, William Monroe Trotter, of Boston, who was quoted as having attempted to cross-examine Mr. Wilson, when the President explained that the question was not a political one, and that he would not be influenced in his decision by the threats of the league to oppose the Democratic Party.

President Wilson informed the delegation that never since he had been in office had he been addressed in such an insulting fashion. He said that if at any time in the future he should consent to receive representatives of the league, that body would have to designate another spokesman ...

The President said the policy of segregation had been enforced for the comfort and best interests of both races in order to overcome friction. He made it clear that he had endeavored in every way to assist the negro race toward its independent development ...

When the President had concluded his remarks, Trotter stepped forward and began questioning Mr. Wilson. He suggested that unless the Administration abandoned the segregation policy the Democratic Party could expect the united opposition of the negro voters in 1916 ...

The mention of votes caused Mr. Wilson to say that politics must be left out, because it was a form of blackmail ... Mr. Wilson urged that he wanted his auditors to understand that it was a human problem and not a political problem …

Once outside Trotter said:

"What the President told us was entirely disappointing. His statement that segregation was intended to prevent racial friction is not supported by facts. For fifty years negro and white employees have worked together in the Government departments in Washington. It was not until the present Administration came in that segregation was drastically introduced."

—From "President Resents Negro's Criticism," *New York Times*, November 13, 1914.

CONSIDER THIS

1. What did Wilson say was his reason for creating the segregation policy? What did Trotter think of this explanation?
2. Do you agree with Wilson that segregation was "a human problem and not a political problem"? Why or why not?

A Poet's Plea

In the first decades of the twentieth century, working-class white people increasingly resented having to compete with black people for jobs. The summer of 1919 brought this resentment to a peak. Race riots broke out around the country, from Texas to Chicago to Washington, DC. This period became known as Red Summer. It was during this time that African American poet Claude McKay

Charles Hamilton Houston, an attorney and educator, provided a strong foundation on which desegregation cases were built through his work with the NAACP.

3 A Solid Foundation

During the two World Wars, black men served in the military and fought to protect their country. These brave men usually fought in segregated units of just black men. However, after the two wars, black soldiers wanted an end to segregation in the military. Their desires would end up having an impact beyond the armed forces.

Segregation in the Military

The acclaimed civil rights lawyer Charles Hamilton Houston served in a segregated unit during World War I. It was his experience in the military that convinced him to become a lawyer. "The hate and scorn showered on us Negro officers by our fellow Americans," said Houston, "convinced me that there was no sense in my dying for a world ruled by them. I made up my mind that if I got through this war I would study law and use my time fighting for men who could not strike back." In other words, he wanted to devote his time to helping black people gain equality in the United States.

During World War II, African American soldiers still struggled with the fact that their nation fought injustice overseas but allowed discrimination at home. Poet Langston Hughes brought the contradiction to America's attention in his 1943 poem "Beaumont to Detroit," in which a black soldier asks why he fights for a democracy that doesn't apply to him. The soldier wonders how long he must struggle for his own freedom at home, and even in the segregated ranks of the army, while helping to free others in Europe.

Beyond the Military

It was not as though these feelings only existed in those who served in the military. Generally, African Americans wanted equal opportunities in education and employment. They wanted this not only in the Jim Crow South but in the North as well. Black people wanted the right to live in any neighborhood, to eat in any restaurant, to attend any concert or event, and to take any seat they wanted.

Activists found different ways to fight the system. Some bravely resisted segregation laws, refusing to tolerate humiliating policies. Others took action through the courts. Regardless of the method, their courage would lead the way to change.

Legal Fights Against Segregation

An exceptional student, Charles Hamilton Houston graduated from Harvard University in the top 5 percent of his class. Houston saw the law as the key to fighting Jim Crow. He became a professor at Howard University, a historically black university. There he trained future black lawyers to join the legal fight against segregation.

As Houston became more well known, the NAACP began to request his help. Its members were determined to overturn *Plessy v.*

Ferguson. By the early 1930s, Houston was the organization's main legal counsel. He decided that the place to begin challenging the "separate but equal" doctrine was public education.

In 1935, a young black man named Lloyd Gaines was denied admission to the law school at the University of Missouri. Gaines was an excellent student and president of his college class. Three years later, Houston and the NAACP took his case to the Supreme Court. The following is the court's decision in the case. It was first in a series of victories that would eventually overturn the separate but equal principle, forcing states to provide educational opportunities that were truly equal for all. Unfortunately, Gaines disappeared before he could ever actually attend the University of Missouri. He has never been found.

> It was admitted on the trial that petitioner's "work and credits at the Lincoln University would qualify him for admission to the School of Law of the University of Missouri if he were found otherwise eligible." He was refused admission upon the ground that it was "contrary to the constitution, laws and public policy of the State to admit a negro as a student in the University of Missouri." It appears that there are schools of law in connection with the state universities of four adjacent States, Kansas, Nebraska, Iowa and Illinois, where nonresident negroes are admitted ...
>
> The basic consideration is ... what opportunities Missouri itself furnishes to white students and denies to negroes solely upon the ground of color ... By the operation of the laws of Missouri a privilege has been created for white law students which is denied to negroes by reason of their race. The white resident is afforded legal education within the State; the negro resident having the same qualifications is refused

it there and must go outside the State to obtain it. That is a denial of the equality of legal right to the enjoyment of the privilege which the State has set up, and the provision for the payment of tuition fees in another State does not remove the discrimination …

We are of the opinion that … [the] petitioner was entitled to be admitted to the law school of the State University in the absence of other and proper provision for his legal training within the State.

—From *Missouri ex rel. Gaines v. Canada, Registrar of the University of Missouri, et al.* No. 57, Supreme Court of the United States, 305 U.S. 337 (1938).

CONSIDER THIS

1. Although the Supreme Court decided in Gaines's favor, it did not go so far as to strike down the separate but equal doctrine established by *Plessy v. Ferguson*. What words in the decision tell us this?
2. How did the state of Missouri bypass federal laws that required it to offer the same educational opportunities to black people that white people enjoyed?

Marian Anderson's Symbolic Performance

On Easter Sunday 1939, a crowd gathered at the Lincoln Memorial to hear the world-famous singer Marian Anderson perform. The event was to have taken place at Constitution Hall. However, the Daughters of the American Revolution (DAR), the organization that ran the hall, refused to let a black singer perform there.

KEY TERMS AND CONCEPTS

From the *Missouri ex rel. Gaines v. Canada* majority opinion:
petitioner The person who makes a formal application to the court, in this case Lloyd Gaines.
provision A legal condition or requirement.

From Walter White's account:
anteroom A waiting room.
askew Tilted or not level.
beneficiary A recipient.
bigotry The intolerance of different people and opinions.
garishly hued Brightly colored.
perturbation Anxiety or uneasiness.
privation The state of lacking basic essentials.
throng A large crowd.

First Lady Eleanor Roosevelt was a member of the DAR. She was also a dedicated opponent of discrimination. Roosevelt demanded that the DAR reconsider its decision. When the organization refused, she publicly gave up her membership. The DAR's policy of discrimination became a topic of national debate.

Roosevelt and other activists arranged for Anderson to perform at the Lincoln Memorial instead. More than seventy-five thousand people arrived to hear Anderson sing. Many more listened to the concert on the radio.

Although the incident had been a painful one for Anderson, her performance was a symbol of achievement for those who struggled

Although Marian Anderson was regarded by many as one of the world's greatest singers, many venues in the United States would not allow her to perform because of her race. She toured widely, however, in Europe and South America, and she gave a public concert at the Lincoln Memorial, shown here, in 1939.

for civil rights. The following is an account of the concert as told by Walter White, the general secretary of the NAACP.

> No member of that audience will ever forget the sight of Miss Anderson emerging from a small anteroom beside Gauden's statue of Lincoln. She was apparently calm, but those of us who knew her were aware of the great perturbation beneath her serene exterior ... The tremendous wave of applause rose from the vast throng, which was silenced only when Miss Anderson gently raised her hand to ask that the concert be permitted to begin. Amplifiers poured out the thunderous chords of the opening bars of "America." Clasping her hands before her Miss Anderson poured out in her superb voice "sweet land of liberty" almost as though it was a prayer.
>
> As the last notes of "Nobody Knows the Trouble I've Seen" faded away the spell was broken by the rush of the audience toward Miss Anderson ... [A] single figure caught my eye in the mass of people below which seemed one of the most important and touching symbols of the occasion. It was a slender black girl dressed in somewhat too garishly hued Easter finery. Hers was not the face of one who had been the beneficiary of much education or opportunity. Her hands were particularly noticeable as she thrust them forward and upward, trying desperately, although she was some distance away from Miss Anderson, to touch the singer. They were hands which despite their youth had known only the dreary work of manual labor. Tears streamed down the girl's dark face. Her hat was askew, but in her eyes flamed hope bordering on ecstasy. Life which had been none too easy for

her now held out greater hope because one who was also colored and who, like herself, had known poverty, privation, and prejudice, had, by her genius, gone a long way toward conquering bigotry. If Marian Anderson could do it, the girl's eyes seemed to say, then I can, too.

—From Walter White, *A Man Called White: The Autobiography of Walter White* (New York: Viking Press, 1948).

CONSIDER THIS

1. Among her selections, Anderson chose to sing "America" ("My Country 'Tis of Thee") and the spiritual "Nobody Knows the Trouble I've Seen." Why do you think she chose these songs?
2. Why was Anderson's appearance at the Lincoln Memorial such an important event?

Thurgood Marshall's Take on Civil Rights

In 1933, Charles Houston asked one of his former students to work for him at the NAACP. "The Association needs another full-time lawyer in the national office," he wrote. "I don't know of anybody I would rather have in the national office than you." The young man's name was Thurgood Marshall, and he accepted Houston's offer.

Five years later, after Houston's resignation, Marshall became the organization's new chief counsel. Down the road, he would become the first African American Supreme Court justice. Like Houston, Marshall firmly believed that it was through the law that people could most effectively fight discrimination. With Marshall, the NAACP won many cases concerning segregation.

The following is a short excerpt from a 1942 speech in which Marshall takes a distinctly different stance than that of early activist Booker T. Washington.

> ... It is necessary and vital to all of us that we continue our program for additional legislation to guarantee and enforce certain of our rights ... We must not be delayed by people who say "the time is not ripe" ... Many people believe the time is always "ripe" to discriminate ...
>
> —From Thurgood Marshall, "The Legal Attack to Secure Civil Rights," July 13, 1942. Speech given at the NAACP Wartime Conference, Chicago, Illinois.

CONSIDER THIS

1. What methods did Marshall believe would be most useful to fight discrimination?

The Ease of Desegregating the Military

On July 26, 1948, President Harry Truman issued an executive order, or a rule issued by the president, to end segregation in the military. The US Air Force immediately complied with Truman's order. It recruited more African Americans, assigning them to units on the basis of skill alone. Talented black soldiers would no longer only be assigned to all-black units. They also would no longer be assigned to the least challenging or exciting posts.

The army and navy resisted integration, or the bringing together of previously segregated groups. However, integration would come to their ranks with or without their cooperation. At the start of the Korean War in 1950, thousands of black men, inspired by Truman's executive order, enlisted in the armed forces. There were too many enlisted black men to fit into existing all-black units. Integration happened naturally. It also happened without the problems that many had anticipated.

By 1953, 95 percent of African American soldiers were serving in integrated units. The following is a television news report from February 27, 1950, reporting on the state of segregation in the armed forces.

> There is some excellent news at hand right now about the normally bad situation of racial discrimination in the Armed Forces. Months ago the President appointed the Fahy Committee to push for equality in the services, and the reports from field surveys are coming in. The Army is just beginning to integrate Negroes and whites in its jobs and schools. But Air Force and Navy have already made some real progress. There are 26,000 Negroes in the Air Force; 71 per cent are now completely integrated—sleeping, studying, working, eating side by side with whites. In a few months, all will be integrated. Field investigators now find the Officer and Service Clubs without discrimination. They find Negroes and whites together at the Air Force swimming pools and dances. The amount of mixing varies from place to place. But it is none the less a remarkable change. And in every place the transition has occurred with remarkably little trouble. Even southern officers who personally do not like it tell the investigators, almost invariably, that the integration is working. There is less friction and not more. At the end of the war [World War II] 95 per cent of the Negroes ... in the Navy were confined to the Steward branch; today only 58 per cent. One can only suggest in this limited space the full story of what is happening. But as one of the

field investigators puts it, what is going on is a kind of quiet social revolution. We feel, he said, that in time this will have an incalculable effect upon the civilian population.

—From the President's Secretary Files, Harry S. Truman Papers (Harry S. Truman Library, Independence, Missouri).

CONSIDER THIS

1. The reporter notes that fewer black soldiers were working in the Steward branch—that is, fewer were working as servants, cooks, or in other less prestigious posts. What significance does this have?
2. According to one field investigator, what effect would desegregation in the military have on the United States?

Jackie Robinson Stays on the Field

Baseball is called the national pastime. However, for the first half of the twentieth century the Major League teams were just another aspect of American life that was closed to black people. In 1947, this changed. The Brooklyn Dodgers gave Jack Roosevelt Robinson the chance to be the first black man to play Major League Baseball since the late 1800s, when the league banned African Americans.

Jackie Robinson had played for the Negro League's Kansas City Monarchs. However, players for the Negro League teams received inferior pay and little recognition for their skills. As Robinson prepared for the Majors, the Dodgers' president, Branch Rickey, warned him that he'd face a great challenge. Robinson would have to be willing to live with ridicule, hostility, and perhaps even death

KEY TERMS AND CONCEPTS

From the television report about desegregation:

incalculable Too great to be measured.

Steward branch People who work as cooks, servants, or as similar support staff in the military.

From Jackie Robinson's account:

crossroads A time at which an important decision must be made.

n***** An offensive term used to refer to black people.

threats. "I'm looking for a ballplayer with guts enough not to fight back," said Rickey.

It would be far from easy, but Robinson was prepared. An excellent athlete, he played four sports at the University of California. He'd reached the rank of second lieutenant in the army. However, like most black men of his day, he'd experienced plenty of discrimination. In fact, he'd been court-martialed, or sent to a court for members of the military, for refusing to sit in the back of a segregated army bus. Ultimately, he was found innocent.

His first days in the league were rocky. However, Robinson went on to become the National League Rookie of the Year. In 1949, he was named the league's most valuable player. Additionally, the Dodgers won six league championships while he was on the team. The following is his recollection of a game played against the Philadelphia Phillies early in his first season.

Jackie Robinson played as both an infielder and an outfielder for the Brooklyn Dodgers from 1947 to 1956. After he left baseball, he was active in the civil rights movement and became a spokesperson for the NAACP.

HISTORICAL SOURCES ON THE CIVIL RIGHTS MOVEMENT

Starting to the plate in the first inning, I could scarcely believe my ears ...

"Hey n***** why don't you go back to the cotton field where you belong?"

"They're waiting for you in the jungles, black boy!" ...

Those insults and taunts were only samples of [what] poured out from the Phillies dugout that April day.

I have to admit that this day, of all the unpleasant days in my life, brought me nearer to cracking up than I ever had been ... I felt tortured ... What ... did Mr. Rickey expect of me? I was, after all, a human being ...

Then I thought of Mr. Rickey—how his family and friends had begged him not to fight for me and my people ... Mr. Rickey had come to a crossroads and made a lonely decision. I was at a crossroads. I would make mine. I would stay.

—From Jackie Robinson and Alfred Duckett, *I Never Had It Made: An Autobiography* (Hopewell, New Jersey: The Ecco Press, 1995). Originally published by G. P. Putnam's Sons, 1972.

CONSIDER THIS

1. Why do you think Branch Rickey chose Robinson despite the difficulties he would face?
2. Why do you think Robinson decided to stay on the team?

The Modern Movement

Although we often consider the civil rights movement to have happened in the 1950s and 1960s, people like Jackie Robinson, Charles Hamilton Houston, and Thurgood Marshall in the 1940s, as well as activists like Ida B. Wells and W. E. B. Du Bois earlier on, paved the way for the modern movement. The created a solid foundation on which the civil rights movement was built.

These six children—(*left to right*) Vicki Henderson, Donald Henderson, Linda Brown, James Emanuel, Nancy Todd, and Katherine Carper—were the motivation for the *Brown v. Board of Education* case, which ended school segregation in 1954.

4 The Dawn of the Modern Movement

In the 1940s and 1950s, the NAACP became increasingly powerful. With additional funds and bright young lawyers, the organization was prepared to take on important discrimination cases. Thurgood Marshall founded its Legal Defense and Educational Fund to bring such cases to trial. He was incredibly successful. In case after case, NAACP lawyers chipped away at legal segregation. They set in motion the most revolutionary years of the civil rights movement. One of these important cases was *Brown v. Board of Education of Topeka*.

Desegregation

In 1954, the Supreme Court gave a landmark decision in *Brown v. Board of Education*. In this case, the court ruled that "separate but equal" was unconstitutional in public schools. Activists and lawyers soon began to apply the decision to segregation in other areas of public life as well. In effect, the court had overturned the 1896 *Plessy v. Ferguson* ruling.

There was a lot of resistance to the *Brown* decision. Although the NAACP continued to work for the admission of black children to all-white schools, the South adopted a policy of "massive resistance." This policy meant that white Southerners would do anything to stop the integration of schools. These actions made the *Brown* decision feel almost meaningless in some places.

Additionally, Southerners created laws to stop the NAACP from operating in their states. Organizations were formed to threaten and challenge civil rights activists at every turn. Worst of all, with increasing legal protection for black people, racist white people turned more and more to violence to maintain segregation.

Brown v. Board of Education of Topeka

The *Brown* case challenged segregated public schools in Topeka, Kansas. A group of parents whose children were denied access to all-white schools fought against the policy. Eventually, the case made its way to the Supreme Court.

Once the case made it to the highest court in the land, Thurgood Marshall and his colleagues argued that restricted facilities, whether equal or not, violated the Fourteenth Amendment. They argued that segregation denied children their civil rights. The Supreme Court agreed.

> Today, education is perhaps the most important function of state and local governments ... Today it is a principal instrument in awakening the child to cultural values, in preparing him for later professional training, and in helping him to adjust normally to his environment. In these days, it is doubtful that any child may reasonably be expected to succeed in life if he is denied the opportunity of an education. Such an opportunity, where the state has undertaken to provide it, is a right which must be made available to all on equal terms.

We come then to the question presented: Does segregation of children in public schools solely on the basis of race, even though the physical facilities and other ... factors may be equal, deprive the children of the minority group of equal educational opportunities? We believe that it does ...

To separate them from others of similar age and qualifications solely because of their race generates a feeling of inferiority as to their status in the community that may affect their hearts and minds in a way unlikely ever to be undone ...

We conclude that in the field of public education the doctrine of "separate but equal" has no place. Separate educational facilities are inherently unequal. Therefore, we hold that the plaintiffs and others similarly situated for whom the actions have been brought are, by reason of the segregation complained of, deprived of the equal protection of the laws guaranteed by the Fourteenth Amendment.

—*Brown v. Board of Education of Topeka* (1954). Supreme Court of the United States, 347 U.S. 483. December 9, 1952, Argued. May 17, 1954, Decided.

CONSIDER THIS

1. Why, according to the *Brown* decision, was the doctrine of "separate but equal" wrong?
2. What laws, according to the court, did the *Plessy* decision violate?

KEY TERMS AND CONCEPTS

From the *Brown v. Board of Education* decision.

deprive To deny someone of something.

inherently Essentially.

Rosa Parks Takes a Stand by Taking a Seat

Civil rights activist Rosa Parks joined the NAACP in 1943. She worked as a youth adviser, helped organize voter registration drives, and was elected secretary of the Montgomery, Alabama, chapter of the NAACP. Her involvement in the civil rights movement became more personal on December 1, 1955.

She was returning home by bus from her job as a seamstress. When the driver asked her to give up her seat to a white passenger, she refused. The front rows on Montgomery's buses were reserved for white passengers. The law required black passengers to give up their seats in the middle section when all the front seats were taken. Parks believed this law was unfair.

On that day in December 1955, she decided to fight it. The driver called the police, and Parks was arrested. This incident led to one of the first major protests of the modern civil rights movement: the Montgomery bus boycott. In this peaceful protest, people boycotted, or stopped using, the buses for nearly a year because of the unconstitutional segregation policy. Here, Parks recounts the experience.

> Having to take a certain section because of your race was humiliating, but having to stand up because a

This photo was taken when Rosa Parks was arrested for refusing to give her seat to a white passenger on a bus in Montgomery, Alabama. This refusal would spark the beginning of the modern civil rights movement.

particular driver wanted to keep a white person from having to stand was, to my mind, most inhumane …

On December 1, 1955, I had finished my day's work as a tailor's assistant … and I was on my way home … The driver asked us [black passengers] to stand up and let him [a white passenger] have those seats …

The driver … asked if I was going to stand up, and I said, "No, I'm not."

And he said, "Well, if you don't stand up, I'm going to call the police and have you arrested."

I said, "You may do that." …

Two policemen came on the bus. One of the policemen asked me … "Why don't you stand up?"

And I asked him, "Why do you push us around?"

—From Henry Hampton and Steve Fayer, *Voices of Freedom* (New York: Bantam Books, 1990).

CONSIDER THIS

1. Why do you think Parks decided not to move that day? If you were in her situation, would you have moved?

Montgomery Bus Boycotts

Civil rights activists in Montgomery went to work immediately after Parks was arrested. The Women's Political Council distributed thousands of flyers announcing a boycott of the city buses. The boycott was meant to take place on the day of Parks's trial. The one-day boycott turned into a 381-day protest. It was led by the Montgomery Improvement Association (MIA) and two young ministers, Martin Luther King Jr. and Ralph Abernathy.

King, the head of the MIA, encouraged protesters to remain peaceful and dignified. The protesters' calm behavior contrasted

During the Montgomery bus boycott, many people walked or carpooled to and from where they needed to go. The protest, which lasted over a year, finally ended when the US Supreme Court declared Montgomery's segregated seating law unconstitutional.

sharply with threats from white people who opposed the boycott. Montgomery's buses remained mostly empty as the black community walked, carpooled, bicycled, or took taxis.

Meanwhile, the MIA took the bus system to court. A judge ordered the buses desegregated. The city refused to obey and took its case to the US Supreme Court. The court agreed with the judge's decision: Montgomery's buses must be integrated. The courage of one woman and the determination of the city's black community had made a tremendous difference. Here is some text from a flyer circulated after the boycott about how to integrate buses.

HISTORICAL SOURCES ON THE CIVIL RIGHTS MOVEMENT

> Within a few days … you will be re-boarding integrated buses. This places upon us all a tremendous responsibility of maintaining … a calm and loving dignity befitting good citizens and members of our Race. If there is violence in word or deed it must not be our people who commit it …
>
> —From Inez Jessie Baskin Papers, Alabama Department of Archives and History, Montgomery, Alabama.

CONSIDER THIS

1. Why do you think the organizers believed it was important that black people were not the cause of "violence in word or deed"?
2. Which do you think is a more effective way to fight discrimination: staging protests such as the Montgomery boycott, or fighting cases in court? Why?

KEY TERMS AND CONCEPTS

From Montgomery Boycott flyer:
befitting Appropriate to.

From Melba Pattillo Beals's account:
bayonet A blade attached to the top of a rifle.

A Governor Ignores the *Brown* Decision

In 1957, massive resistance to integration met another challenge in Arkansas. The NAACP had won a court order requiring the admission of nine black students to Central High School in Little Rock. When the Little Rock Nine, the group of black students, tried to attend classes on September 23, riots broke out.

Governor Orval Faubus brought in the state's National Guard. He did this to block the Little Rock Nine from entering the school. This act of defiance forced the federal government to take action. President Dwight Eisenhower took control of the state's National Guard. He required the National Guard to take orders from him instead of Faubus. Eisenhower also sent US Army troops, forcing the state to comply with the court order.

Clearly, *Brown* was only the first step in ending segregation in schools. In the following account, Melba Pattillo Beals, one of the Little Rock Nine, recalls September 25, 1957. This was the day when one thousand army paratroopers, members of the army who are prepared to jump from planes with parachutes, arrived to ensure the integration of Central High.

> As we neared the school, I could hear the roar of a helicopter directly overhead … I could see that armed soldiers and jeeps had already blocked off certain intersections approaching the school. Closer to the school, we saw more soldiers and many more hostile white people … , lining the sidewalk and shaking their fists. But for the first time I wasn't afraid of them …
>
> Sarge said we should wait in the station wagon because the soldiers would come for us. As I looked around, I saw a group of uniformed men walking toward us, their bayonets pointed straight up …

Despite the tensions, eight of the Little Rock Nine attended Central High School for the entire year. A senior during the 1957–1958 academic year, Ernest Green became the first African American to graduate from Central High.

Rifles at their sides, their faces stern, the soldiers ... surrounded us in a protective cocoon ...

Step by step we climbed upward [on the stairs of the school]—where none of my people had ever before walked as a student.

—From Melba Pattillo Beals, *Warriors Don't Cry: A Searing Memoir of the Battle to Integrate Little Rock's Central High* (New York: Pocket Books, 1994).

CONSIDER THIS

1. How do you think you would have felt getting ready for school that first day if you were a member of the Little Rock Nine?
2. How do you think Beals felt walking where none of her "people had ever before walked as a student"?

A White Student Responds

How did the white students at Central High feel about integration? Some of the students simply wanted their lives to get back to normal. As one student told the *New York Times*, "If the parents would just go home and leave us be we'd work this thing out for ourselves." One of the Little Rock Nine, Ernest Green, agreed: "Things would be better if only the grown-ups wouldn't mix in. The kids have nothing against us."

Regardless of how the students felt, the adults could not be convinced. Governor Faubus closed Little Rock high schools at the end of the school year to prevent further integration. The schools remained throughout the 1958–1959 school year. Regardless of the governor's actions, the feelings of some Central High students

All over the country, not just in the South, people fought against the inequalities black people faced. For instance, this photo shows a protest in Chicago in 1960.

5 *Fighting Back Through Peaceful Protest*

As previously mentioned, people had differing opinions about how to get civil rights for black people. The NAACP and Thurgood Marshall fought for equality through trying to change laws that affected black people. However, other civil rights activists looked to a different method: direct action, or protests, marches, and boycotts. With the success of the Montgomery bus boycott, Martin Luther King Jr. emerged as a powerful voice in the civil rights struggle. In 1957, he joined with other ministers and activists to found the Southern Christian Leadership Conference (SCLC). Its goal was to support the NAACP's efforts through nonviolent, public protests. These protests were designed to bring about quick and effective change.

Martin Luther King Jr.'s Approach

While studying to become a minister, King was introduced to the idea of peaceful protest as a means to fight oppression. He learned about Mahatma Gandhi, the great Indian leader who had opposed British rule of India through nonviolent resistance. As a result of Gandhi's efforts, India achieved independence in 1947. King believed that Gandhi's technique represented the best path for black Americans. Soon the concept of nonviolence inspired activists around the country, especially in the South. "You can struggle without hating," said King, "you can fight without violence."

King delivered his famous "I Have a Dream" speech at the Lincoln Memorial in August 1963, the same place Marian Anderson sang almost three decades earlier.

Unfortunately, although many civil rights activists remained true to the principle of nonviolence, their opposition did not. Civil rights workers were jailed, beaten, humiliated, and even killed.

Nonviolence

Gandhi's principles had been the guiding force behind the Montgomery bus boycott. After its success, friends encouraged King to travel to India and witness firsthand the results of Gandhi's campaign. With his wife, Coretta, King made the visit in 1959. The trip only deepened his commitment to nonviolence. In the following passage, King explains the concept of nonviolent protest.

> It is necessary that the mass action method be persistent and unyielding ... All history teaches us that like a turbulent ocean beating great cliffs into fragments of rock, the determined movement of people ... demanding their rights always disintegrates the old order.
>
> —From Martin Luther King Jr., "The Social Organization of Non-Violence," *Liberation*, October 1959.

CONSIDER THIS

1. What did King mean by "a turbulent ocean beating great cliffs"?

Woolworth's Sit-Ins

King's theory of nonviolence spread throughout the movement. On February 1, 1960, four black freshmen from the North Carolina Agricultural and Technical State University sat down at an all-white lunch counter at the Greensboro Woolworth's,

KEY TERMS AND CONCEPTS

From Martin Luther King Jr.'s "The Social Organization of Non-Violence":
disintegrate To break down.
persistent Continuing to follow a course of action.
turbulent Unsteady or agitated.
unyielding Not giving up.

From the letter to the president of Woolworth's:
rancor Bitterness.
resentment Bitterness about unfair treatment.

a general store. They asked to be served. The waitress responded, "We don't serve colored here." The young men waited, remaining seated at the counter until the store closed. The next day, twenty more students joined them. On the third day, white students from a local women's college took part in the protest as well. Soon the sit-ins, a form in peaceful protest where people sit or stay at a certain place, spread across the state.

Within two months, students had staged sit-ins in fifty-four cities in nine states, at a variety of public places. All the while, the students obeyed a few simple rules: "Do show yourself friendly on the counter at all times. Do sit straight and face the counter. Don't strike back or curse back if attacked. Don't laugh out. Don't hold conversations. Don't block entrances."

Segregationists assaulted the student protesters. Sometimes people threw food or insulted them. Other times, they pulled the students from their chairs, arrested them, or even attacked

It is important to note that white people could not be served while peaceful protesters occupied seats at segregated counters, which meant businesses would lose money.

them with tear gas and police dogs. Still, the students knew that if they stayed true to the principle of nonviolence, no one could rightfully criticize them.

The sit-ins set in motion a new phase in the civil rights movement. During this phase, black and white students played an important role. Later that year, the students who had participated in the sit-ins formed the Student Nonviolent Coordinating Committee (SNCC) to help organize more direct-action protests and involve people in the movement at the local level. The following is a letter written by the leaders of the Greensboro sit-in to the president of Woolworth's.

> We the understated are students at the Negro college in the city of Greensboro. Time and time again we have gone into Woolworth stores of Greensboro. We have bought thousands of items at hundreds of the counters in your stores. Our money was accepted without rancor or discrimination and with politeness

> toward us, when at a long counter just three feet away our money is not acceptable because of the color of our skins. This letter is not being written with resentment toward your company, but with the hope of understanding ...
>
> We are asking that your company take a firm stand to eliminate discrimination. We firmly believe that God will give courage and guidance in the solving of this problem.
>
> —From Ezell Blair Jr., David Price, Joseph McNeil, David Richmond, and Franklin McCain (sit-in leaders), to the president of F. W. Woolworth & Company, letter of February 1, 1960. In Miles Wolff, ed., *Lunch at the Five and Ten: The Greensboro Sit-Ins* (New York: Stein and Day, 1970).

CONSIDER THIS

1. Why do you think black people were permitted to purchase items at Woolworth's but not eat at the lunch counter?
2. Why did protest leaders set rules for the students to follow at the sit-ins?

John Lewis and the Freedom Riders

Although change was slow, change was happening. In 1960, the Supreme Court ruled that it was illegal to segregate public transportation that traveled between states. This ruling included ticket counters, waiting rooms, and restaurants in train and bus stations.

Not surprisingly, Southern states didn't want to comply. Leaders from the Congress of Racial Equality (CORE), a civil rights organization made up of black and white members, decided to protest continued segregation on buses. In the spring of 1961, thirteen CORE members took a "Freedom Ride" from Washington, DC, to New Orleans.

Divided into two groups traveling on separate buses, they purchased their tickets in Washington without an issue. But the farther south they traveled, the more intense the Freedom Ride became. In the following account, John Lewis, one of the younger Freedom Riders, explains what happened when they reached Rock Hill, South Carolina. Lewis went on to become chairman of the SNCC and an organizer of voter registration drives. In 1986, he won a seat in the US House of Representatives.

> As Al Bigelow and I approached the "white" waiting room in the Rock Hill Greyhound terminal, I noticed a large number of white guys hanging around the pinball machines in the lobby. Two of these guys were leaning by the doorjamb to the waiting room. They wore leather jackets, had those ducktail haircuts and were each smoking a cigarette.
>
> "Other side, n*****," one of the two said, stepping in my way as I began to walk through the door. He pointed to a door down the way with a sign that said "colored."
>
> I did not feel nervous at all. I really did not feel afraid.
>
> "I have a right to go in here," I said, speaking carefully and clearly, "on the grounds of the Supreme Court decision in the *Boynton* case."

Not everyone was pleased with the desegregation of interstate public transportation. For instance, segregationists attacked Freedom Riders John Lewis (*left*) and James Zwerg (*right*) in Alabama.

I don't think either of these guys had ever heard of the *Boynton* case. Not that it would have mattered ...

The next thing I knew, a fist smashed the right side of my head. Then another hit me square in the face. As I fell to the floor I could feel feet kicking me hard in the sides. I could taste blood in my mouth.

At that point Al Bigelow stepped in, placing his body between mine and these men, standing square, with his arms at his sides.

It had to look strange to these guys to see a big, strong white man putting himself in the middle of a fistfight like this, not looking at all as if he was ready to throw a punch, but not looking frightened either.

They hesitated for an instant. Then they attacked Bigelow, who did not raise a finger as these young men began punching him. It took several blows to drop him to one knee.

At that point several of the white guys by the pinball machines moved over to join in. Genevieve Hughes [a white Freedom Rider] stepped in their way and was knocked to the floor.

That finally brought a reaction from a police officer who had stood by and witnessed the entire scene. He stepped in, pulled one guy off us and said, "All right boys. Y'all've done about enough now. Get on home."

Within minutes more police arrived, including a sympathetic officer who asked if we wanted to press charges. I was back on my feet by then, woozy and feeling stabs of sharp pain above both eyes and in my ribs. My lower lip was bleeding pretty heavily ...

We said no to the offer to press charges. This was simply another aspect of the Gandhian perspective. Our struggle was not against one person or against a small group of people like those who attacked us that morning. The struggle was against a system, the system that helped produce people like that ...

The attack that day—the first time blood was drawn on the Freedom Ride—did exactly what we wanted it to do. It drew attention.

—From John Lewis, *Walking with the Wind: A Memoir of the Movement* (New York: Simon and Schuster, 1998).

CONSIDER THIS

1. Why didn't the Freedom Riders press charges against the attackers?
2. Why did the Freedom Riders want to attract attention?
3. Do you think you would have responded like Lewis to being attacked? Do you think you would have responded like Bigelow to witnessing an attack? Why or why not?

KEY TERMS AND CONCEPTS

From John Lewis's memoir:

***Boynton* case** In 1960, the Supreme Court ruled that interstate buses and related facilities—bus terminals, restrooms, etc.—must be desegregated *(Boynton v. Virginia)*.

From Governor Ross Barnett's statement:

abhor To think of with disgust.

federalized Made to serve the national government.

sovereignty of this ... state The state's power or authority.

vestige A trace.

Governor Ross Barnett and the Integration of Ole Miss

In 1962, a young man named James Meredith hoped to transfer from an African American college and spend his senior year at "Ole Miss," the all-white University of Mississippi in Oxford, Mississippi.

Predictably, when he applied, the school resisted. Its decision was supported by Governor Ross Barnett, an enthusiastic segregationist. When Meredith tried to register for classes in September 1962, Governor Barnett traveled to the university so that he could personally deny Meredith entrance to the school. "No school will be integrated in Mississippi while I'm governor," Barnett promised.

As had happened a few years earlier in Little Rock, the federal government and the president—this time, John F. Kennedy—had

These two young boys, Dwight (*left*) and Floyd Armstrong (*center*), were denied admission to an all-white school in Birmingham, Alabama, by state troopers in 1965.

6

The Battle for Birmingham

In 1960, *New York Times* reporter Harrison Salisbury visited Birmingham, Alabama, to investigate its race relations. He wrote, "Whites and blacks still walk the same streets. But the streets, the water supply and the sewer system are about the only public facilities they share." Birmingham was simultaneously the most segregated and the most racially violent city in the country. Salisbury wrote about how racism and segregation were "reinforced by the whip, the razor, the gun, the bomb, the torch, the club, the knife, the mob, the police, and many branches of the state's apparatus." In other words, the state supported or allowed the sort of violence and racism that unfolded in Birmingham.

The Birmingham Campaign

The town's police chief, Eugene "Bull" Connor, was famous for his strict segregationist beliefs. He ordered his men to break up all black political meetings and punished white people who were friendly to African Americans. The manager of the city's bus terminal had been arrested twice for obeying the orders to desegregate the buses.

It was in Birmingham that Martin Luther King would launch his 1963 campaign. King, Ralph Abernathy, and other leaders from the SCLC began communicating with members of Birmingham's black community. They trained citizens in the techniques of nonviolence.

At the invitation of Fred Shuttlesworth, the city's leading civil rights activist, King and other SCLC leaders arrived in Birmingham on April 2, 1963, to initiate Project C (for "confrontation"). Also known as the Birmingham campaign, the activists staged protests, sit-ins, marches, and boycotts all over the city. These protests would last for a couple of months. During this time, the police would become increasingly violent in response to these peaceful protests. They would use dogs, nightsticks, and high-pressure water hoses to attack protesters, even children who marched.

The violence in Birmingham caught the nation's attention. It ignited civil rights demonstrations throughout the country.

Letter from a Birmingham Jail

Early in the Birmingham campaign, Bull Connor attempted to halt the protests by getting a court order demanding that the civil rights activities cease. With this court order in force, Martin Luther King had a choice to make. To continue demonstrations in Birmingham, he would have to defy the law. Yet the law was exactly what he was trying to uphold through peaceful protest. Ultimately, as King told reporters, he felt the protests in Birmingham had "reached the point of no return."

On Good Friday, he led some fifty marchers toward city hall, singing hymns along the way. Hundreds black citizens stood by in support. Connor was furious. He ordered his squad with its police dogs to arrest the demonstrators. Cameras and news reporters captured the event on film. The nation watched police load King into a police van. The next day, several of the town's white clergymen took out an advertisement in the *Birmingham News*. They said the protests were "unwise and untimely."

"We do not believe that these days of new hope are days when extreme measures are justified in Birmingham," the clergymen wrote. King responded from jail. He wrote a letter in the margins of a newspaper and on toilet paper. His response, "Letter from a Birmingham Jail," explained why the struggle against racism could not wait.

> Perhaps it is easy for those who have never felt the stinging dart of segregation to say, "Wait." But when you have seen vicious mobs lynch your mothers and fathers … and drown your sisters and brothers … then you will understand why we find it difficult to wait …
>
> —From Martin Luther King Jr., "Letter from a Birmingham Jail." April 16, 1963.

CONSIDER THIS

1. Give an example of another time that black activists were cautioned to be patient and wait for the situation to get better.

The Children's Crusade

When King was freed on bail, he saw that the demonstrations were losing support. Many of the city's black citizens were in jail. Those who weren't feared arrest or worse. Black businessmen complained of losing business. Black religious leaders called for caution. With few adults eager to protest, SCLC leaders decided to recruit children in the cause.

On May 2,1963, more than a thousand children and teenagers marched in the streets of Birmingham. They sang hymns and chanted freedom slogans. Bull Connor was unmoved. He gathered school buses to haul hundreds of young people to jail. A thousand more students assembled the next day. Connor called in police

It was not uncommon for protesters to be attacked by policemen wielding nightsticks, firehoses, and dogs.

dogs and firefighters to attack the terrified crowd. The firefighters aimed hoses at the children. These high-pressured hoses were strong enough to rip clothing and throw children to the ground and over parked cars. They even drew blood.

Television cameras recorded the confrontation. Around the nation, Americans watched in outrage as dogs lunged at children. Viewers saw human beings hurled against walls by the powerful blast of a fire hose. They witnessed police attacking demonstrators with nightsticks. Horrified, leaders in Washington, DC, knew they had to act.

The Justice Department sent the assistant attorney general to negotiate peace between protesters and the city. Knowing the protests would continue and the economy would suffer, the city eventually agreed. The following is a portion of the statement released by Shuttlesworth, King, and Abernathy describing the agreement made with the city of Birmingham.

> Responsible leaders of both Negro and white communities of Birmingham, being desirous of promoting conditions which will ensure sound moral, economic and political growth of their city, in the interest of all citizens of Birmingham, after mutual consideration and discussion of the issues relating to the recent demonstrations in the city, have agreed to the following:
>
> 1. The desegregation of lunch counters, rest rooms, fitting rooms, and drinking fountains, in planned stages within the next ninety days.
>
> 2. The upgrading and hiring of Negroes on a nondiscriminatory basis throughout ... Birmingham. This will include the hiring of Negroes as clerks and salesmen within the next sixty days ...

3. Our movement has made arrangements for the release of all persons on bond or their personal recognizance. Our legal department is working with further solutions to this problem.

4. Through the Senior Citizens Committee or the Chamber of Commerce, communications between Negro and white to be publicly re-established within the next two weeks [in order to] prevent the necessity of further protest demonstrations.

—From Fred L. Shuttlesworth, Martin Luther King Jr., and Ralph Abernathy, joint statement of May 10, 1963. Published in the *New York Times*, May 11, 1963.

CONSIDER THIS

1. Can the terms of this agreement be considered a victory for the SCLC and the protesters?
2. Do you agree with the terms of the agreement? Should the protesters have demanded anything else?

Kennedy's Promise

After the election of President John F. Kennedy in 1960, civil rights supporters, both black and white, gained a new sense of hope. Kennedy had actively wanted the support of black people. Additionally, his youth and energy held the promise of great change. But at the beginning of his term, Kennedy became all too familiar with the powerful presence of Southern leaders in Congress. They blocked any attempt at civil rights legislation.

KEY TERMS AND CONCEPTS

From the joint statement:
bond A legal agreement, especially involving a repayment.
recognizance A promise someone makes to observe a specific condition, like a bond.

From President John F. Kennedy's "Report to the American People on Civil Rights":
constructive Useful or productive.
discord A disagreement between people.
prudently Carefully.
redress A solution for wrongdoing.
repressive Limiting someone's freedoms.

At the same time, it was a critical moment in US history. The nation was on the edge of war with the Soviet Union, present-day Russia. Tensions between the two countries ran high. Kennedy had little time to focus on civil rights issues. However, the alarming events in Birmingham changed this. The following is Kennedy's "Report to the American People on Civil Rights" of June 11, 1963, about one month following the agreement in Birmingham.

> We preach freedom around the world, and we mean it, and we cherish our freedom here at home, but are we to say to the world, and much more importantly, to each other that this is the land of the free except for the Negroes; that we have no second-class

citizens except Negroes; that we have no class or caste system, no ghettoes, no master race except with respect to Negroes?

Now the time has come for this Nation to fulfill its promise. The events in Birmingham and elsewhere have so increased the cries for equality that no city or State or legislative body can prudently choose to ignore them.

The fires of frustration and discord are burning in every city, North and South, where legal remedies are not at hand. Redress is sought in the streets, in demonstrations, parades, and protests which create tensions and threaten violence and threaten lives.

We face, therefore, a moral crisis as a country and as a people. It cannot be met by repressive police action. It cannot be left to increased demonstrations in the streets. It cannot be quieted by token moves or talk. It is time to act in the Congress, in your State and local legislative body and, above all, in all of our daily lives.

It is not enough to pin the blame on others, to say this is a problem of one section of the country or another, or deplore the fact that we face. A great change is at hand, and our task, our obligation, is to make that revolution, that change, peaceful and constructive for all ...

I am, therefore, asking the Congress to enact legislation giving all Americans the right to be served in facilities which are open to the public—

> hotels, restaurants, theaters, retail stores, and similar establishments ...
>
> I am also asking the Congress to authorize the Federal Government to participate more fully in lawsuits designed to end segregation in public education ...
>
> But legislation ... cannot solve this problem alone. It must be solved in the homes of every American in every community across our country.
>
> —From "Report to the American People on Civil Rights," President John F. Kennedy, The White House, June 11, 1963. From the John Fitzgerald Kennedy Library, Boston, Massachusetts.

CONSIDER THIS

1. According to Kennedy, were civil rights laws important? What did he believe they could achieve? What could they not achieve?
2. Do you think Kennedy supported the demonstrations and protests?
3. How could the problems Kennedy described "be solved in the homes of every American"?

The Murder of Medgar Evers

Around midnight on June 11, 1963, the night President Kennedy gave his historic civil rights speech, Medgar Evers was fatally shot in his driveway in Jackson, Mississippi. Evers knew his life was in danger. It had been for nearly a decade.

In 1954, the NAACP had decided to send representatives into the Deep South. For years, the organization had practically given up hope in Mississippi. Black people in the state were afraid to even talk about the NAACP. But in an effort to gain new members and renew its work where it was most needed, the NAACP selected activists such as Evers to set up new offices in Deep South cities.

Evers had two main responsibilities: to recruit members and to investigate violence against black people. Evers was effective, and his success drew attention. That attention made him a target of hate and violence. In his travels around the state, he was followed, threatened, beaten, and mocked. However, the attacks did not stop him until white people murdered him. His wife, Myrlie, recounts the night of his murder below. It was an event that electrified the civil rights movement in Mississippi and beyond.

> Medgar had told me that President Kennedy was speaking on civil rights that night ... The children, who had heard about the president's address to the nation, planned to watch it with me ...
>
> It was a moving speech, the most direct and urgent appeal for racial justice any President of the United States had ever made. It moved me and gave me hope and made what Medgar was doing seem more important than ever before ...
>
> Darrell heard the car first. "Here comes Daddy." ... I roused myself as the tires reached the gravel driveway, stretched, and then heard the car door close ...
>
> A shot rang out, loud and menacing. The children, true to their training, sprawled on the floor ...
>
> I flew to the door, praying to be wrong. I switched on the light. Medgar lay face down at the doorway, drenched with blood.

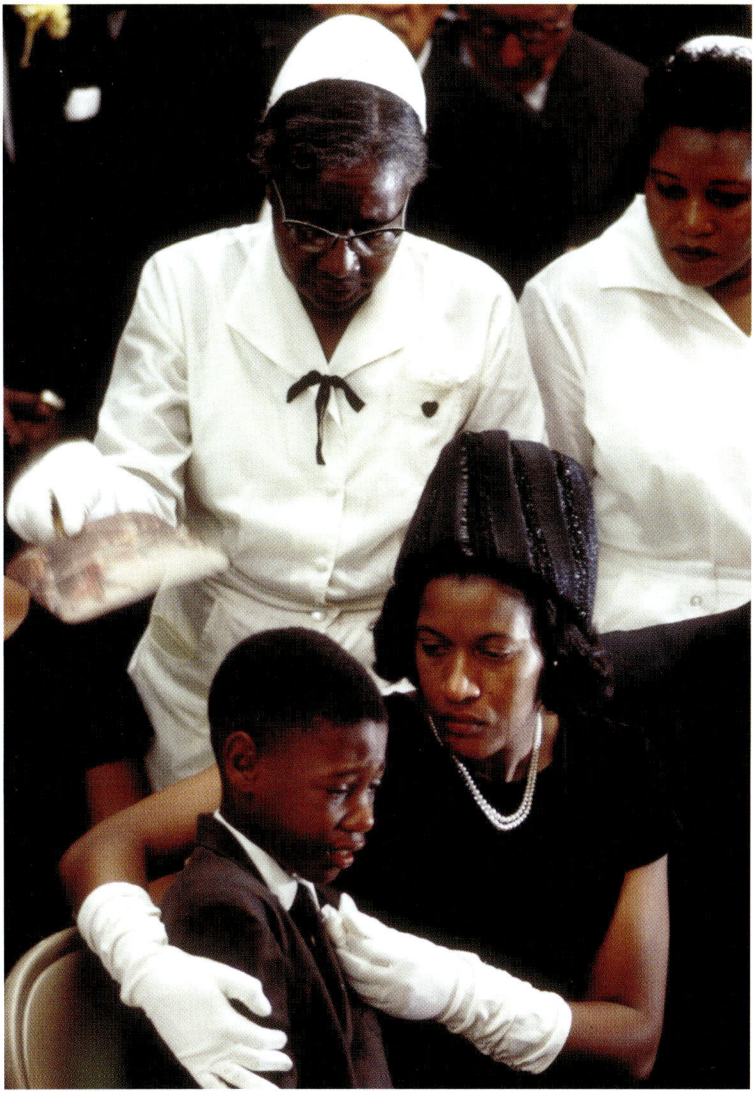

Myrlie Evers comforts her son Darrell at the funeral of her husband, civil rights leader Medgar Evers. Despite her loss, she would continue to be an active member of the NAACP, serving on its board until 1998.

—From Myrlie Evers, *For Us, the Living* (Jackson, Mississippi: Banner Books, University Press of Mississippi, 1967).

CONSIDER THIS

1. Why did the NAACP send people such as Evers into the Deep South, knowing it would be dangerous?
2. Why were these activists willing to go?

Waves of Peace and Tragedy

On August 28, 1963, more than two hundred thousand Americans marched down the National Mall to gather at the Lincoln Memorial in Washington, DC. At the time, it was the largest peacetime gathering in US history. It was the March on Washington for Jobs and Freedom. Though some, including President Kennedy, feared the day might end in violence, it was a peaceful celebration.

On June 19, true to his promise, President Kennedy had introduced a civil rights bill into Congress. The sea of people that swelled before the Lincoln Memorial gathered in support of the bill. They hoped that their sheer numbers would convince members of Congress to pass it. The marchers held placards telling of their dreams for a better future: "We March for Effective Civil Rights Laws Now!" "We Demand Voting Rights Now!" "If You're Not Against Discrimination, You're Not for Freedom!" A day filled with inspiration in song and words ended with one of the most memorable speeches in US history. Martin Luther King delivered his "I Have a Dream" speech. The day ended in hope. The civil rights movement was making a difference.

Less than a month after the March on Washington, tragedy shattered the hope inspired by the gathering. It was a Sunday morning in Birmingham. Sunday school was in session. A powerful bomb exploded in the basement of the all-black Sixteenth Street Baptist Church. It killed eleven-year-old Denise McNair and three fourteen-year-olds, Addie Mae Collins, Carole Robertson, and Cynthia Wesley.

Despite the tragedies that followed the August 1963 March on Washington, hope still remained on the horizon.

These four little girls, killed in the Sixteenth Street Baptist Church bombing, were not the only innocent victims of the violence ignited by the civil rights movement; however, their deaths shook the nation.

It was no accident that the bombing took place at the Sixteenth Street Baptist Church. The church was the staging ground for the Children's Crusade earlier that year. The incident fueled riots in the city as citizens took to the streets. A Montgomery newspaper recounted the violence of the riots.

> At police headquarters reports of death and violence kept coming in late into the night.
>
> A 16-year-old Negro boy was reported shot and killed by a policeman ...
>
> Another Negro boy was reported slain while riding a bicycle.
>
> A firebomb was reported thrown at a Negro home ...

—From Arthur Osgood, "Racial Tension Mounts in Birmingham after Four Killed in Church Bombing," *The Montgomery Advertiser*, September 16, 1963.

CONSIDER THIS

1. Why do you think riots broke out following the church bombing?
2. Do you think the people responsible for the bombs were ever caught and tried for their crimes? Why or why not?

A Shift in Power

Toward the end of 1963, the spirit of hope and commitment that had been born at the March on Washington was fading quickly. Another painful blow came with the terrible news of John F. Kennedy's assassination in November of the same year. Activists wondered if there would be any hope of the civil rights bill becoming law without him.

The vice president, Lyndon B. Johnson, became president after Kennedy's death. Johnson was from Texas, a Southern state that made no secret of its racist policies.

President Lyndon B. Johnson signed the Civil Rights Act of 1964 into law surrounded by civil rights leaders like Martin Luther King Jr.

7 Change on the Horizon

On November 27, 1963, five days after Kennedy's death, President Lyndon B. Johnson addressed Congress and the nation for the first time. He promised to pass the civil rights bill in Kennedy's memory. Johnson was a former member of Congress. He was no stranger to the legislative process. He used his know-how and talent to get the bill passed. Believing that no politician and no American could ignore the issue of civil rights, he would accept no compromises. The bill was passed without changes.

The Civil Rights Act of 1964

On February 10, 1964, the House of Representatives passed the civil rights measure by 290 to 130 votes. Still, everyone knew the real battle would be in the Senate, where Southerners had killed nearly every piece of civil rights legislation. But with Johnson as an ally and the nation's desire to honor the memory of President Kennedy, civil rights leaders hit the Capitol with an impressive campaign to get the bill passed. The Senate listened.

On June 19, one year from the day Kennedy had proposed the act, the Senate passed the most important piece of civil rights legislation in the nation's history. The Civil Rights Act of 1964 made it illegal to discriminate against someone because of his or her race, color, religion, sex, or national origin. The following is a selection from President Johnson's address before signing the bill, on July 2, 1964.

> This is a proud triumph. Yet those who founded our country knew that freedom would be secure only if each generation fought to renew and enlarge its meaning ...
>
> We believe that all men are created equal. Yet many are denied equal treatment.
>
> We believe that all men have certain unalienable rights. Yet many Americans do not enjoy those rights.
>
> We believe that all men are entitled to the blessings of liberty. Yet millions are being deprived of those blessings—not because of their own failures, but because of the color of their skin.
>
> The reasons are deeply imbedded in history and tradition and the nature of man. We can understand—without rancor or hatred—how this all happened.
>
> But it cannot continue. Our Constitution, the foundation of our Republic, forbids it. The principles of our freedom forbid it. Morality forbids it. And the law I will sign tonight forbids it ...

The purpose of the law is simple.

It does not restrict the freedom of any American, so long as he respects the rights of others.

It does not give special treatment to any citizen.

It does say the only limit to a man's hope for happiness, and for the future of his children, shall be his own ability.

It does say that ... those who are equal before God shall now also be equal in the polling booths, in the classrooms, in the factories, and in hotels, restaurants, movie theaters, and other places that provide service to the public ...

We will achieve these goals because most Americans are law-abiding citizens who want to do what is right ...

So tonight I urge every public official, every religious leader, every business and professional man, every workingman, every house-wife—I urge every American—to join in this effort to bring justice and hope to all our people—and to bring peace to our land.

—From *Public Papers of the Presidents of the United States: Lyndon B. Johnson, 1963–64*. Volume II, entry 446, pp. 842–844 (Washington, DC: Government Printing Office, 1965).

CONSIDER THIS

1. Johnson quotes the Declaration of Independence, saying that all men have "certain unalienable rights." Did the Founders believe these rights applied to everyone who lived in the United States?
2. Johnson says Americans should "understand—without rancor or hatred" how racism and discrimination came to be a part of life. How might civil rights activists have felt about this?
3. How did the Civil Rights Act of 1964 "renew and enlarge" the meaning of freedom?

Freedom Summer

The passage of the Civil Rights Act of 1964 did not mark the end of the movement. There was still work to be done. For one thing, the act failed to address fully the right of black citizens to vote. Ready for action, activists set their sights on ensuring that African Americans would be able to cast their votes safely and participate in the democratic process, even in the Deep South.

Between 1961 and early 1964, hundreds of thousands of new black voters had been registered. This increase was due in large part to the efforts of the Voter Education Project. It was a joint effort of several civil rights organizations. One state, however, managed to resist the project completely: Mississippi. Only 5 percent of eligible black people in Mississippi were registered to vote. Some counties did not have a single black voter.

White people in the state claimed black people simply didn't want to vote. This was not the case. To register, African Americans had to take tests, and white government employees determined whether they had passed. Potential voters could be denied registration for neglecting to dot an *i* or cross a *t*. Sometimes they

KEY TERMS AND CONCEPTS

From President Lyndon B. Johnson's speech:

deeply imbedded Firmly rooted.

law-abiding citizens People who follow a country's laws.

unalienable Unable to be taken away from a person.

From Les Johnson's account

abstract Existing as a thought or idea but not really experienced.

deteriorating Falling apart.

From Fannie Lou Hamer's testimony:

blackjack A piece of metal wrapped with leather that is used as a weapon.

All of this is on account of us wanting to register, to become first-class citizens, and if the Freedom Democratic Party is not seated now, I question America, is this America, the land of the free and the home of the brave where we have to sleep with our telephones off of the hooks because our lives be threatened daily because we want to live as decent human beings, in America?

—From Fannie Lou Hamer, "The Testimony of Fannie Lou Hamer at the 1964 Democratic Convention," July 22, 1964.

CONSIDER THIS

1. What makes Hamer's speech effective?
2. What elements are most disturbing about Hamer's story?

A More Militant Stance

In the later years of the civil rights movement, a more radical voice emerged. It was the voice of Malcolm X. Unlike Martin Luther King, Malcolm X did not believe nonviolence was the answer to ending discrimination. He thought that black people must achieve equality "by any means necessary." Sometimes, these means might include violence.

Malcolm X was a member of the Nation of Islam. It was a religious movement founded on the idea of black separatism. He firmly supported black separatists' principle that black and white people could never live together peacefully.

By the mid-1960s, many African Americans had grown disappointed with the slow pace of change. To dissatisfied African Americans, Malcolm X provided an alternative. After

Malcolm X, born Malcolm Little, encouraged black people to be proud and to preserve their black identities in the United States. His beliefs and principles continued to inspire young black people after his assassination.

his assassination in February 1965, his ideas gained increasing popularity as more young activists began to take a militant approach to equal rights.

The following is an excerpt from a 1964 speech by Malcolm X, given before an Ohio audience. It provides a very different perspective on civil rights. Keep in mind that Malcolm X lived in the North, in New York City, and he was speaking to a Northern audience.

> The question tonight, as I understand it, is "The Negro Revolt, and Where Do We Go From Here?" or "What Next?" In my little humble way of understanding it, it points toward either the ballot or the bullet …
>
> 1964 threatens to be the most explosive year America has ever witnessed. The most explosive year. Why? It's also a political year. It's the year when all of the white politicians will be back in the so-called Negro community jiving you and me for some votes. The year when all the white political crooks will be right back in your and my community with their false promises, building up our hopes for a letdown, with their trickery and their treachery, with their false promises which they don't intend to keep. As they nourish these dissatisfactions, it can only lead to one thing, an explosion; and now we have the type of black man on the scene in America today … who just doesn't intend to turn the other cheek any longer …
>
> It's time now for you and me to become more politically mature and realize what the ballot is for; what we're supposed to get when we cast a ballot;

KEY TERMS AND CONCEPTS

From Malcolm X's Speech

jiving Talking nonsense; deceiving.

treachery Betrayal.

From the description of the Selma march:

prod To poke.

retreat To withdraw or move back.

skitter To move quickly.

unobstructed view A clear view.

and that if we don't cast a ballot, it's going to end up in a situation where we're going to have to cast a bullet. It's either a ballot or a bullet.

—From Malcolm X, "The Ballot or the Bullet." Speech delivered April 3, 1964. Republished in George Breitman, ed., *Malcolm X Speaks* (New York: Grove Weidenfeld, 1965).

CONSIDER THIS

1. Explain in your own words what Malcolm X meant by "the ballot or the bullet."
2. What was Malcolm X urging his audience to do?
3. How do you think people would have responded if he gave his speech in the South?

Violence Erupts in Selma, Alabama

In January 1965, Martin Luther King and the SCLC began a series of protests in Selma, Alabama. They wanted to bring national attention to the issue of voting rights. They planned a 50-mile (80-kilometer) march from Selma to Montgomery. Once in Montgomery, they would present Governor George Wallace with a petition of grievances, or a list of complaints.

Wallace said the march would not be tolerated. He issued an order to prohibit it, but the protesters began the march as planned. Police cars lined their route. Approaching the Edmund Pettus Bridge, the protesters saw state troopers waiting for them on the other side with gas masks, hard hats, and billy clubs, or short sticks used as weapons. "You have two minutes to turn around and go back to your church," said the commander. Within a minute, he gave orders to attack: "Troops advance!"

The first 10 or 20 Negroes were swept to the ground screaming, arms and legs flying and packs and bags went skittering … Those still on their feet retreated.

The troopers continued pushing, using both the force of their bodies and the prodding of their nightsticks.

A cheer went up from the white spectators lining the south side of the highway …

Suddenly there was a report, like a gunshot, and a gray cloud spewed over the troopers and the Negroes.

"Tear gas!" someone yelled.

The cloud began covering the highway. Newsmen, who were confined by four troopers to a corner 100 yards away, began to lose sight of the action. But before the cloud finally hid it all there were several seconds of unobstructed view. Fifteen or twenty nightsticks could be seen through the gas flailing at the heads of the marchers.

—From Roy Reed, "Alabama Police Use Gas and Clubs to Rout Negroes," *New York Times*, March 7, 1965.

CONSIDER THIS

1. The governor and other white people in Alabama believed that force against the protesters was the only way to keep them from gaining power. Are there issues with this strategy? What are they?

The Voting Rights Act

Alarmed by the violence, the nation reacted with outrage to the events in Selma. Within little more than a week, President Johnson had sent a voting rights bill to Congress. This bill would eliminate all illegal barriers to the right to vote. "This time, on this issue," said Johnson, "there must be no delay, no hesitation, and no compromise with our purpose." Signed into law on August 6, 1965, the Voting Rights Act prohibited election laws that denied or restricted the voting rights of minorities. The following is an excerpt from President Johnson's remarks prior to signing the act.

> This law covers many pages. But the heart of the act is plain. Wherever, by clear and objective standards, States and counties are using regulations, or laws, or tests to deny the right to vote, then they will be struck down. If it is clear that State officials still intend to discriminate, then Federal examiners will be sent in to register all eligible voters. When the prospect of discrimination is gone, the examiners will be immediately withdrawn.
>
> And, under this act, if any county anywhere in this Nation does not want Federal intervention it need only open its polling places to all of its people.
>
> This good Congress, the 89th Congress, acted swiftly in passing this act. I intend to act with equal dispatch in enforcing this act …
>
> But only the individual Negro, and all others who have been denied the right to vote, can really walk through those doors, and can use that right, and

can transform the vote into an instrument of justice and fulfillment.

So, let me now say to every Negro in this country: You must register. You must vote. You must learn, so your choice advances your interest and the interest of our beloved Nation. Your future, and your children's future, depend upon it, and I don't believe that you are going to let them down.

If you do this, then you will find, as others have found before you, that the vote is the most powerful instrument ever devised by man for breaking down injustice and destroying the terrible walls which imprison men because they are different from other men.

—From President Lyndon B. Johnson, Remarks in the Capitol Rotunda at the Signing of the Voting Rights Act, August 6, 1965. *Public Papers of the Presidents of the United States: Lyndon B. Johnson, 1965.* Volume II, entry 394 (Washington, DC: Government Printing Office, 1966).

CONSIDER THIS

1. Compare Johnson's words to Malcolm X's "The Ballot or the Bullet" speech. Are there any similarities?
2. Once the Voting Rights Act was passed and enforced, who would hold the responsibility for ensuring that black Americans voted?

The black power movement was increasingly popular among students. The movement celebrated black beauty as well as African heritage and cultures.

The Beginning of the End

The passage of the Voting Rights Act is thought by many to mark the beginning of the end of the civil rights movement. Serious issues began to divide activists. Young members of the SNCC and CORE had begun to question the principle of nonviolence. Some even objected to the participation of white people in what they saw as an African American struggle. As one young activist announced, "We don't need any more white phonies and liberals invading our movement."

These strong feelings gave rise to the black power movement. This movement focused on blacks' self-reliance, or the ability to take care of oneself without the help of others, and racial dignity. In 1966, Huey Newton and Bobby Seale founded the Black Panther Party. The organization believed self-defense was justified in all attempts to bring social and economic equality to the United States. The Panthers believed black people had a right to defend themselves against police brutality and other forms of anti-black violence. They often patrolled black neighborhoods to ensure that African Americans were not the victims of police brutality. Both black power supporters and the Panthers found inspiration in the work of Malcolm X.

Violence ultimately did become a part of the movement, especially in cities. Five days after the signing of the Voting Rights Act, a six-day riot broke out in Watts, a black neighborhood in Los Angeles. The following year would see even more chaos, as riots erupted in more than one hundred US cities. President Johnson created a commission, or a committee with a particular focus, to study the outbreak of urban violence. The commission concluded that civil rights legislation had not done enough to help black Americans. It warned that the nation "is moving toward two societies, one black and one white—separate and unequal."

More moderate activists also continued their work in the second half of the 1960s. Martin Luther King turned his attention to fighting poverty in black communities across the nation. In 1968, he planned another major protest, the Poor People's March. It would take place in Washington on April 28. The march did take place, but without its leader. On April 4, 1968, Martin Luther King was assassinated at a motel in Memphis, Tennessee. Within hours of his death, violence raged in cities across the country. The peaceful civil rights movement had come to an end.

The Legacy of the Movement

Did the movement achieve all that it could have? The legislation passed and court rulings made during the civil rights era certainly have made a great difference in the nation's future. However, many believe the legislation wasn't enough. As Dwight Eisenhower said at the height of the Little Rock Nine crisis, "You cannot change people's hearts merely by laws." He went on to say that laws do express the conscience of a nation. In that way, the civil rights movement made America see that too many of its people were denied the freedom promised by democracy. The movement could not change every American's heart, but it did begin the process. There is still so much further to go, even today.

Although the official movement came to a close in 1968, black people still struggle to enjoy their civil rights in the United States. After the tumultuous presidential election of 2000, black voters in Florida accused election officials of denying them the right to vote.

Similarly, there have also been charges of resegregation. Since the 1980s, black and white people in many areas have been attending separate schools again. This is not because of discrimination laws but because of school districts and communities in which people live. Often times, wealth disparities, or differences, cause some of this segregation. This trend, like segregation in the early twentieth century, has not been confined to the South. In 2011, the most segregated school districts in the United States were in the Northeast.

Perhaps worst of all, racial violence against black people has continued in the United States. In 1998, three Texas racists brutally murdered a black man, James Byrd. They beat him, chained him to the back of a pickup truck, and dragged him for several miles. More recently, Dylann Roof, a young white supremacist, murdered nine African Americans in a 2015 mass shooting at the Emanuel African Methodist Episcopal Church in Charleston, South Carolina.

Hate and intolerance in the United States continue to be an issue. It will continue to take brave men and women of all races to not only combat hate and violence but to make changes to ensure a better, safer future for all.

CHRONOLOGY

1865 The Thirteenth Amendment, outlawing slavery, is ratified.

1868 The Fourteenth Amendment, guaranteeing African Americans citizenship and legal protections, is ratified.

1870 The Fifteenth Amendment, granting African American men the right to vote, is ratified.

1875 Congress passes the Civil Rights Act of 1875, protecting black people's rights to enjoy public facilities and serve on juries. The law is ultimately overturned by the US Supreme Court in 1883 (*Civil Rights Cases*).

1896 The Supreme Court rules that the segregation of railway cars is constitutional (*Plessy v. Ferguson*), solidifying the "separate but equal" principle.

1909 The NAACP is founded.

1919 Red Summer occurs.

1938 The US Supreme Court rules that it is unconstitutional to deny Lloyd Gaines admission to the University of Missouri (*Missouri ex rel. Gaines v. Canada*).

1948 President Harry Truman issues Executive Order 9981, which leads to the desegregation of the military.

1954 The US Supreme Court rules that segregated public schools are unconstitutional (*Brown v. Board of Education of Topeka*), reversing the idea of "separate but equal."

1955 Two white men murder Emmett Till. Rosa Parks is arrested. The Montgomery bus boycott starts.

1957 Martin Luther King Jr. and other activists form the Southern Christian Leadership Conference. The Little Rock Nine start attending Central High School.

1960 Four black freshmen stage a sit-in at a Greensboro, North Carolina, lunch counter. Hundreds of similar protests follow.

1961 The SNCC is organized. The Freedom Riders leave DC.

1963 Project C begins in Birmingham, Alabama. President Kennedy delivers his civil rights address. Medgar Evers is assassinated. The March on Washington for Jobs and Freedom occurs. The Sixteenth Street Baptist Church in Birmingham is bombed. President Kennedy is assassinated.

1964 President Johnson signs the Civil Rights Act of 1964. Freedom Summer occurs.

1965 Malcolm X is assassinated. State troopers attack peaceful protesters at the beginning of a march from Selma to Montgomery. President Johnson signs the Voting Rights Act

1966 The Black Panther Party is founded.

1968 Martin Luther King is assassinated. President Johnson's commission on civil rights determines that the country is moving toward a more separate existence. The civil rights movement dissipates.

GLOSSARY

activism Participation in activities to bring attention to a cause.

boycott To refuse to financially support a business or service as a form of protest.

civil rights Personal freedoms guaranteed to someone who is a citizen of a country.

civil rights movement The organized struggle for justice and equality for African Americans in the United States (1954–1968).

constitutional Legal based on the principles outlined in the US Constitution.

delegate A representative at a convention or meeting.

direct action Protests, strikes, and boycotts, designed to achieve a goal quickly.

dissenting opinion A written statement explaining why a justice, or multiple justices, disagree with a court's ruling.

executive order A law or rule issued by the president that does not require action from Congress.

integration Incorporating people from different races or backgrounds into society as equals so that all people have equal access to facilities and services.

legislation The laws that are made or passed by a lawmaking body, such as Congress.

lynch To kill someone, especially by hanging, for a crime he or she is suspected of having committed without giving him or her a trial.

majority opinion A written statement explaining why a court made its ruling or decision.

minstrel shows Theatrical performances in the nineteenth and early twentieth centuries in which white people wore black makeup on their faces and acted like black people; the shows often reinforced stereotypes and prejudices that white people held about African Americans.

Reconstruction Amendments The Thirteenth, Fourteenth, and Fifteenth Amendments. These amendments, in order, abolish slavery, provide equal protection to all citizens under the law, and give black men the right to vote.

Reconstruction Era The period (1865–1877) following the Civil War (1861–1865) when Confederate states were reorganized into the Union and the United States was trying to rebuild the South.

segregation The separation of a race, class, or other group by means of discriminatory laws and policies.

sit-in A form of peaceful protest where individuals refuse to leave a place until their demands are met.

suffrage The right to vote.

unconstitutional Illegal based on the principles outlined in the US Constitution.

FURTHER INFORMATION

Books

Machajewski, Sarah. *The Freedom Rides: The Rise of the Civil Rights Movement*. Lucent Library of Black History. New York: Lucent Books, 2018.

McCormick, Anita Louise. *Rosa Parks and the Montgomery Bus Boycott*. Spotlight on the Civil Rights Movement. New York: Rosen Young Adult, 2018.

Rhuday-Perkovich, Olugbemisola. *The Civil Rights Movement*. Step into History. Danbury, CT: Childrens' Press, 2018.

Walker, Paul Robert. *Remember Little Rock: The Time, the People, the Stories*. Remember. Washington, DC: National Geographic Childrens' Books, 2015.

Woodson, Jacqueline. *Brown Girl Dreaming*. New York: Puffin Books, 2016.

Websites

The Civil Rights Movement

http://www.cnn.com/EVENTS/1997/mlk/links.html

This CNN website provides a timeline that further details events related to the civil rights movement.

Library of Congress: Civil Rights History Project
https://www.loc.gov/collections/civil-rights-history-project/about-this-collection

This website provides more first-hand accounts of the civil rights movement through interviews with people involved in the struggle.

We Shall Overcome:
Historic Places of the Civil Rights Movement
https://www.nps.gov/nr/travel/civilrights

This National Park Service website provides an interactive map that allows you to learn more about the sites and places important to the civil rights movement, such as Selma and William Monroe Trotter's house in Massachusetts. Additionally, it provides a general overview of the movement.

Videos

Fourteen Civil Rights Legends
Who Paved the Way for Us All
https://www.youtube.com/watch?v=4d5EjvCB_HA

This video provides a brief overview of some of the most prominent civil rights leaders and their legacies.

Martin Luther King Jr.'s "I Have A Dream" Speech
https://www.youtube.com/watch?v=_IB0i6bJIjw

This video discusses the March on Washington for Jobs and Freedom and Martin Luther King Jr.'s involvement, including his powerful speech.

Organizations

American Civil Liberties Union
125 Broad Street, 18th Floor
New York NY 10004
(212) 549-2500
Website: https://www.aclu.org

Formed in 1920, this organization works to secure and protect the rights every US citizen is given by the US Constitution and laws.

Center for Civil and Human Rights
100 Ivan Allen Jr. Boulevard
Atlanta, GA 30313
(678) 999-8990
Website: https://www.civilandhumanrights.org

This organization focuses on empowering people to protect everyone's human rights through sharing the history of the civil rights movement and sharing the stories of those fighting for their human rights around the world in its museum.

**The Martin Luther King Jr.
Center for Nonviolent Social Change**
449 Auburn Avenue, NE
Atlanta, Georgia 30312
(404) 526-8900
Website: http://www.thekingcenter.org

Founded by Coretta Scott King, Martin Luther King Jr.'s wife, after his death in 1968, this organization is focused on education and social change.

Mississippi Civil Rights Museum
222 North Street, Suite 2205
Jackson, MS 39201
(601) 576-6800
Website: https://mcrm.mdah.ms.gov

This museum showcases Mississippi's role in the civil rights movement. It sheds a special light on the stories of people who fought and struggled for equality.

National Association for the Advancement of Colored People
4805 Mt. Hope Drive
Baltimore MD 21215
(410) 580-5777
Website: https://www.naacp.org

Founded in 1909, the NAACP is one of the nation's largest and oldest civil rights organizations. It strives to end race-based discrimination and to ensure equality for all.

National Civil Rights Museum: At the Lorraine Motel
450 Mulberry Street
Memphis, TN 38103
(901) 521-9699
Website: https://www.civilrightsmuseum.org

This Smithsonian-affiliated museum at the Lorraine Motel, where Martin Luther King Jr. was assassinated, provides history and information concerning the civil rights movement and its effects on the country.

INDEX

Page numbers in **boldface** refer to images.

INDEX

ABOUT THE AUTHORS

Chet'la Sebree is a writer, editor, and researcher from the Mid-Atlantic. She has received degrees in English and writing from the University of Richmond and American University. She has worked on several books about US history, including the Courting History series for Cavendish Square Publishing. Her research focus is early American history.

Elizabeth Sirimarco published her first book in 1990. Since that time, she has written books on a range of topics such as Thomas Jefferson and the Cold War. A graduate of the University of Colorado at Boulder, she also earned a degree in Italian from the Università per Stranieri in Siena, Italy. In addition to writing, Sirimarco works as an editor and occasionally enjoys the opportunity to work as an Italian translator. She and her husband David, a photographer, live with a very large dog and a very small cat in Denver, Colorado.